WHEN WE HAD WINGS

THE GRIPPING STORY OF AN ORPHAN IN
JANUSZ KORCZAK'S ORPHANAGE.
A HISTORICAL NOVEL

TAMI SHEM-TOV

ISBN 9789493276772 (ebook)

ISBN 9789493276758 (paperback)

ISBN 9789493276765 (hardcover)

Publisher: Amsterdam Publishers, The Netherlands

info@amsterdampublishers.com

When We Had Wings is part of the series WW2 Historical Fiction

Copyright English text © Tami-Shem Tov, 2023

First published by kinneret-Zmora-Dvir publishing house

Translated to Japanese: Tokyo, Fukuinkan, 2015

Translated from the Hebrew by Shula Werner

Hebrew title: *Ani Lo Ganav*

Author image: Ido Perez

1

WARSAW, POLAND. 1935

Until they broke my legs no one could run faster than me. When I sped through the streets people stared in amazement and wondered, *What was that?* And when they realized I was only a boy, they hoped I would one day compete in the Olympic Games and bring honor and pride to us all. Indeed, thanks to my amazing speed, I won races, eluded street gangs and bullies, and also managed to grab and run, to steal. I was proud of my running but not of stealing. I especially hated being called *a thief and the son of a thief*, but that was the truth.

Once, when I was a small child, I took three tin toy soldiers from some boy. That was the first time I can remember stealing. My sister Mira, who is ten years older than me, caught me playing with those silly soldiers and made me give them back. The boy hadn't even missed them – he had about a hundred of them. But Mira didn't relent. She even demanded I apologize to the boy's mother – what did she have to do with it? – and that was the worst part of it all.

The second thing I stole was a book. I don't know why I decided to steal it; perhaps because it had a beautiful cover or perhaps because of the nice lady who was reading it to her little boy. He wore a striped sailor suit and looked like a doll in a shop window. He wasn't even listening to his mother – he didn't look interested at all. They were sitting on a bench on the edge of a park and I ran around there for about ten minutes. After a while the lady put down the book to wipe her son's nose, so I dashed towards them, snatched the book and ran home. Except for a few boring parts, it was quite a nice book. Later I gave it to a girl in my neighborhood.

I never stole another book, but I did steal plenty of newspapers. I would snatch them from the pockets of men's jackets or from under people's arms in a crowded street or a railroad station. I read the newspapers from front to back, because if I didn't make good use of what I had stolen, it seemed such a waste, and that made me feel bad.

I usually returned the newspapers to the boys who sold them on the streets, shouting out the headlines, so that they could sell them again. Sometimes I was given a few coins for the newspapers I returned. It seemed fair. Besides, I never actually stole from a newspaper boy.

Most of all I stole food: bread, butter, cheese, sausages, sweets, cakes, biscuits, bagels, fruit, vegetables and even fish from the fishmongers and often from people's shopping baskets. I once stole pancakes from a plate in a restaurant. I had almost succeeded in escaping through the open door when someone stuck out his leg and tripped me. Two men got up quickly, grabbed me and, with their mouths still full of herring, slapped me hard on the face.

Of course, that was unpleasant, even painful, but it was nothing compared to what I felt when my legs were broken. It happened at the orphanage, the so-called Shelter. Some older children set me a trap and caught me stealing. Then they knocked me down and kicked my legs over and over again, while the headmaster stood by and watched. After a while he told them to stop. Before I lost consciousness I heard him say, "Let's see him run now!"

It took me quite a while to become strong enough to run away from that orphanage and drag myself through the snow to my sister's place. For several months I lay on a mattress on the floor and never left the house. I didn't want anybody to see me limping.

Still, word got round. Every now and then someone would stroll through the yard and shout, "Janek the lame thief" or "Let's see you beat me in a race now, you limping thief!" My sister Mira pretended not to hear and acted as though she was busy with her baby, but she heard everything and knew she was to blame, for it was she who had sent me to that terrible place.

That is why I couldn't believe it when one day, while she was scrubbing the baby's diapers on the washboard, she said, "Janek, I have heard about a wonderful orphanage." I turned my back on her and smiled bitterly at the impossible combination of the words "wonderful" and "orphanage". I might be a lame thief, I thought, but she was a traitor. And a liar.

2

———

I loved Mira more than anyone in the world and never had a bad thought about her. She was like a mother to me. Our mother died soon after I was born, so I can't remember her at all. I met our father only twice, when he came home from prison on a day release. Later we were told that he died there.

After our mother died we stayed with our grandmother who lived in a small flat in one of the poorest districts of Warsaw. But she also passed away when I was about six years old. Although we had some distant relatives in a faraway village and even one or two in the city, we never heard from any of them. My sister said that we didn't need them; we had each other. She had promised our mother and then our grandmother that she would take care of me as if I were her own child.

We continued to live in grandma's flat. It was a tiny dark place, the walls were damp and we had to put pots and basins on the floor to collect the water dripping from the leaking roof. We didn't have any electricity or running water either. The place was no palace, but it was ours and no one could tell us what we should or should not do there.

Mira was a seamstress, just like Mother and Grandma had been before her. She worked at home, mending clothes and curtains. Later, she worked for a rich and kindly lady. She liked working there, and I too was happy during those days. In the mornings I went to school where I did not encounter any difficulties at all. I could write easily without any mistakes, probably because of all the newspapers I'd read. When I was called upon to recite out loud I did so, here again without making any mistakes. And I always did my homework. That is why the teacher never made fun of me, never reprimanded or struck me. I got on well with the other children because I was a fast runner, good at sports and everyone wanted me on their team.

In the afternoons I just roamed around or played in the street. In the evenings I would run to the nice lady's place, which was in a good neighborhood with tall houses and green gardens. I was usually invited into the back kitchen, where a sour-faced servant gave Mira and me some hot soup with fried meat patties or some herring on bread with butter. I didn't mind *Sour-face*, as we called her, glaring at me in disgust. In those days we didn't expect grown-ups to be nice to us kids. We were always noisy and made a mess, we disappointed them, and we cost them money. In short, I understood that we bothered them. I sometimes wondered why people brought children into the world in the first place; perhaps, if they were rich, they wanted a child as a toy for their amusement; someone to recite poems to aunts and uncles.

After supper with we would go home. If Mira felt like it and was not too tired, we raced each other. Mira was very fast in those days, though sometimes she would laugh for no reason and that slowed her down. When we got home we sat down together to do my homework. Mira would say that, thanks to me, she too was learning – which was good, because she had had to leave school after second grade.

And then the rich lady fired her.

That evening, after a long game of catch, I came to the lady's house all filthy and sweaty in order to go home with Mira. But this time the maid did not invite me in. Her sour face peeped through a crack in the doorway and she said, "Don't come here ever again, you dirty urchin, and as for your sister, she had better find a husband of her own!" Then, before slamming the door, she spat on the pavement.

I ran home and found Mira sweeping the floor.

"Why did *Sour-face* say you should find a husband of your own"? I asked.

Mira mumbled that the nice lady's husband had bought her sweets wrapped in colorful paper and left her little notes on her sewing machine saying that she was pretty. Suddenly I saw her with different eyes. I had never asked myself whether she was pretty or not. I just never looked at her that way. Mira told me that the lady found the notes and was very angry. "She should have fired him, not me!" she declared, leaning on the broom, "but that's not the way it works. It's easier to think that I'm the one to blame."

"Why?"

"Never mind," she said biting her nail. "You wouldn't understand anyway."

The summer sunlight streamed through the window and Mira had the urge to go for a run, so she could decide what to do next. Every evening throughout that summer till the beginning of the winter, Mira ran for hours at a time. During the day she looked for work but could not find anything. We began selling our belongings to buy food and coal to heat the house. There was almost nothing left; we even sold the sheets, and I stopped going to school as Mira couldn't pay the school fees. She never inquired how I brought home apples and potatoes, beets and cabbage and even cheese. At last, when she was almost desperate because she couldn't find a job, she did what *Sour-face* had told her to do: she found herself a husband.

And then everything went wrong.

Staszek – who earned some money by buying and selling all kinds of junk, second-hand clothes and kitchen utensils – moved in with us. Immediately after the wedding he acted as though he owned the place. When he wasn't giving orders, he just talked and talked and talked. I never met anyone who talked as much as Staszek. Usually he talked about politics. At times, he was a *Zionist* and claimed that all of us, all the Jews in the world, should go to Palestine.

At other times he surprised us by making speeches about social justice and Jewish-Polish culture. Then, as if he belonged to the Jewish workers' party, the *Bund*, he declared that Poland was our fatherland and that we had to preserve our culture and our language, Yiddish. Sometimes he decided that he liked the Hassidic way of life and that living as an ultra-Orthodox Jew would be especially suitable for me. He would pester me then for not growing side locks, or going to the synagogue and for not studying at one of the free religious schools.

What an idiot.

Staszek used to end his bombastic speeches with stories about his two brothers; one of them had emigrated to America and the other to Palestine. No wonder neither of them took Staszek with him.

Sometimes I went to work with him. Unwillingly, I dragged the junk along, loaded the wagon, carried things up the stairs and listened to his tiresome explanations. But when he blamed me for stealing a broken clock that he wanted to repair and sell, I stopped working with him.

About that time Mira had a baby. She was upset because the baby cried all the time. Staszek too was irritable and short-tempered. People probably got tired of him and his junk. Anyway, he often lost his temper and scolded me and blamed me for everything. He said I gave the family a bad name, running about all the time like an idiot instead of working to help feed the family. He also called me names: good for nothing, spoilt brat, trash, thief, criminal. I heard him say to my sister that I was totally worthless, like a clock beyond repair. He didn't want to upset her so he added that it was not her fault, because she had done all she could. It was the street that had corrupted me. I am sure he said he didn't want me around Shmulik, their baby, so that he wouldn't be influenced by me and become a thief as well. He probably said that while he was chewing on the potatoes I stole for them. What a hypocrite.

Once I talked back to him and he slapped my face. I thought Mira would throw him out for doing that, but she just kept quiet. Later they had a huge row, and when they made up, it was me they threw out. They sent me to an orphanage, the so-called *Shelter* – a totally inappropriate name; the place was more like a prison, a prison for children. When I was there I thought a lot about my father – he had been in prison for such a long time, he even died there. But I don't want to think of that now.

3

Finally, I agreed to go to another orphanage; the one Mira said was wonderful. As if I had a choice.

Mira and I went there by streetcar. I used to jump onto street cars and ride for free, but this time Mira paid for two tickets. She left the baby with a neighbor. I looked out of the window onto the street and imagined I was racing the streetcar, galloping like a horse, all covered in sweat, my heart beating like crazy.

"I know you're mad at me, Janek," said Mira. "But this time, I promise you, everything will be just fine. Everyone wants to go to this place, even children who are not orphans. It wasn't easy to get you in there, believe me."

She told me that she had gone to the lady who fired her. She waited till the husband left for work and then knocked on the door. It took the lady quite a while to agree to let her in and speak to her. While Mira was talking, I noticed that one of the passengers standing nearby kept looking at us.

"Remember the morning a few weeks ago when I woke you up and asked you to take care of Shmulik?" Mira asked.

I didn't answer. Of course I remembered. How could I forget? She had shouted at me and forced me to get up, because I usually slept until noon.

"That morning I went to see the lady because I just didn't know what to do with you anymore. I needed her help. She has connections, she knows some important people. Besides, she is smart and knows what to do when things get out of hand. She remembers you well. It broke her heart when she heard what had happened to you."

Mira said I was very lucky. At the very time the lady was making inquiries and pulling strings, one single place had became available in a Jewish orphanage, directed by Janusz Korczak, a writer and children's doctor. The nice lady sent Mira a note with a date and time when she should go to see the director, the *Doctor* as she called him, and his co-worker, Miss Steffa.

"I was very impressed with them," Mira said. We were silent for a while and then Mira resumed her story. She told me that in Dr. Korczak's orphanage there were also girls. "That means it's a good place, doesn't it?"

"What do you mean by that?" I tested her.

"I don't know," Mira was less confident now. "Still, it seems to signify something good."

"Why?" I feigned not to understand.

Mira shrugged.

I didn't tell her that she was right, for if there were girls it couldn't be a rough place like the Shelter. In really bad places such as prisons, women are kept separate from men. There were no girls in the Shelter. God knows what would have happened to them there.

"Listen," Mira said with enthusiasm. "In Korczak's orphanage the children themselves run the place. The grown-ups are there just to help and supervise. Can you believe it?"

No, I couldn't. Either someone had put one over on her, or she didn't know the difference between what was going on in her head and what was real.

"And what else?" I asked scornfully.

"They have central heating there, and electric lights. It's clean there, no lice or fleas. You won't have any festering bites on your head. Remember how you used to scratch them? And there are no bad smells. I saw the dormitories – two large halls, one for the boys and the other for the girls. And the beds are all covered with clean white sheets. Only in the lady's house did I ever see such white sheets, pulled tight with no creases." She spread her fingers to show how tight the sheets were spread.

"I even went to look at the toilets. They are inside the building, not outside in the yard like in our home. And so clean, absolutely sparkling!"

She began to speak as if she were in a dream, just like she used to do when I was small and she was telling me a bedtime story. "They serve food three times a day, bread, meat, cheese, milk, soup, cocoa. Even herring."

I was hungry. I wanted to believe her, of course I did. But then she said, "They have a special lift only for food! The food is brought up from the kitchen to the dining room in the lift!"

Well, really! That was too much. I thought that Mira had caught her husband's disease of babbling. At least she had some imagination. He couldn't have invented lifts for food.

Then she began talking about Miss Steffa and the Doctor. Both had kind eyes, she said. Steffa was tall, broad-shouldered and strict, Korczak was strong and gentle.

"*Strong* and *gentle*, how do they go together?" I asked.

She didn't answer my question; she just said that she had never met such a nice person as the doctor. She took the baby with her when she went to meet Korczak and Miss Steffa. Shmulik cried the whole time and Mira was afraid they would be angry and throw her out, but that was not what happened. The doctor asked her permission to examine Shmulik.

"Would you believe it?"

It seems that Korczak spent quite a while examining Shmulik. He examined his tummy, his throat, his ears, his arms and legs.

"Have you noticed that Shmulik doesn't cry as much lately?" Mira asked, smiling. "The doctor explained that he had an aching tummy and showed me how to hold him after meals to ease his discomfort. It's so simple. What a pity nobody explained it to me before!" she whispered, mainly to herself.

People got on and off the streetcar. Everybody seemed troubled;

nobody looked happy. I stared at the man who kept looking at us, especially at Mira. Perhaps she really is pretty, just like the nice lady's husband wrote. The man noticed my stare and finally looked away.

Mira came closer and whispered, "I told the Doctor that you were beaten at the Shelter and that you have a slight problem walking. I didn't tell him that you limp. He might not want cripples in his place." And as if that wasn't enough she added, "I also didn't tell him that you're a thief."

She put her hand on my knee. Her fingernails were bitten to the bone. I pushed her hand away. "Oh Janek," she sighed. I cursed her. She was shocked and turned her face to the window. She did not want me to see her crying. I didn't care. I had enough of her – of her, of Staszek who had spoilt everything for us, and of her baby who cried all the time. I decided that today, whether I stayed at that wonderful orphanage of hers or ran away, I would say my last good-bye to Mira. I thought that I'd probably end up living on the streets, perhaps even die there. And that would teach her a lesson.

4

The house at 92 Krochmalna Street was surrounded by a yard and enclosed by a stone wall. I had passed the house several times before, when I could still run, but had never gone beyond the gate. Now I limped towards a broad, three storied building with a small attic and a large window on the roof. "There was no garden at the Shelter, was there?" Mira said, pointing proudly to the plants in the large courtyard as if she had planted them herself.

A strong wind blew the leaves off the tall trees. The door to the house opened and a large woman dressed in black came towards us. When she was almost in front of us, and without slowing down, she began talking.

"Welcome Janek, pleased to meet you. I am Miss Steffa. I'll talk to you later. Meanwhile please go in. The Doctor is waiting for you."

We went into what seemed to me to be a palace, a large clean house full of light. I followed Mira through an open corridor into a large hall – on one side was a library, and on the other side there were some small tables and chairs. Between the second and the third floor there were two mezzanines with low banisters. On one of the landings stood a large shiny grand piano.

The windows were all large and wide. I noticed them because at the Shelter the windows were very small and close to the ceiling. It was always dark there, even when the sun shone brightly. Here, not only were the windows tall, but the ceiling was also lofty. Our footsteps rang out in the quiet building. There was no other sound because it was still early and the kids were all at school.

Mira knocked on a door at the end of the corridor. A voice called: "Come in," and Mira entered the room with me at her side. I was sure that Korczak would look like the rabbi who taught young boys in the cheder in our neighborhood – perhaps because Mira had said he had a beard, or perhaps because this was a Jewish orphanage. But Korczak didn't look at all like the rabbi. He wore a light green doctor's coat; his beard was smooth and cut close to his chin. His spectacles were round and he had a shiny bald head. And, as Mira had said, he had twinkling eyes and the smile of a man with a kind heart. I reminded myself that all that meant nothing. A pleasant smile and kind eyes can be deceiving and kindheartedness but an illusion.

That's what went through my mind as I followed Mira towards a large desk which almost filled the tiny room. Janusz Korczak sat between the desk and a bookcase. I realized immediately that he noticed my limp. Mira also saw him watching the way I dragged my leg.

"His leg keeps improving," Mira lied as she sat herself in the chair opposite him. "Perhaps it's worse than usual this morning because it's really getting cold. Bones get hard in the cold. Isn't that true, Mister Doctor?"

I remained standing and looked hard into his eyes, daring him not to pity me. I hate being pitied. I barked at him, "Actually, I had it coming. I was caught stealing."

"A child takes a newspaper from a grown man and that is what they do to him?!" Mira said, trying to repair the damage, and added, "But it is getting better all the time... yes, his walking is improving."

I could hear children outside running and shouting.

"First, my walking is not getting better," I declared wickedly, enjoying contradicting her and ruining her effort. "And secondly, I didn't steal a newspaper only once. I stole it every day. I also stole apples. The truth is, I am a thief, and until they broke my legs I was hardly ever caught because I could run like the devil!"

Mira laid her head on the table and began to cry softly.

The noise from outside got louder and the Doctor's face turned red. "They should be sent to prison!" he shouted, and his look was no longer kind and gentle. "Why do they work with children? Why? If all they want is to break them, body and soul?!"

"Who?" I asked, surprised.

"Those criminals at the Shelter! They are criminals, and are surely worse than thieves!"

Mira lifted her head and stared at him in surprise.

"The worst is that they are allowed to behave like that and we can do nothing to stop them. If we send a letter, if we take them to court, we'll be laughed at. They'll say, 'What else should they do? The boy is a thief, how will he learn otherwise?!'"

"Don't grown-ups ever remember that they too were once children?" I exclaimed – even I was surprised at my question.

"Janek, you're talking nonsense," Mira retorted, embarrassed.

"Some people hardly remember," answered the Doctor, "and others remember all the time. But I believe that those who are cruel to children are trying very hard to forget their own childhood."

I immediately understood that he belonged to the kind of people who always remember.

There was a long silence, and then the Doctor asked Mira, "And how is little Shmulik?"

"Much better," she replied, wiping her tears. She was delighted that Korczak remembered her crying baby, even remembered his name, but it wasn't him that she wanted to talk about now. She just wanted to know whether the Doctor would accept me into his orphanage, even after he found out that I was a lame thief.

"What about Janek?" she asked.

"Nobody steals here. It's not worth it," the Doctor replied without any anger. "The children's court can expel a child for stealing. Besides, there are plenty of apples and newspapers here. If anyone wants something or needs it, he just asks for it. If it's possible, he is given what he wants; if not – then not."

"Did you hear, Janek?" Mira remarked unnecessarily.

Suddenly a big bell started ringing. Korczak stood up and announced, "I'm hungry, what about you?" Of course we were hungry. But we were too shy to say so. The Doctor invited Mira to stay for lunch. To my disappointment she accepted.

Some of the children ran towards the Doctor. One little boy clung to his legs and a little girl stretched out her hand to be kissed, as if she was a queen. He smiled, patted some children's heads, kissed some on the forehead and talked to others for a few moments. I was very confused. Grown-ups didn't act like this towards children, certainly not towards children who were not their own, and certainly not towards poor children. Normally we were treated as if we were wild animals that needed to be tamed.

The Doctor led us to a table covered with a clean tablecloth and set with cutlery and water jugs. Five children were already seated at the table and we joined them. I was sure that in a minute Korczak would leave and go to a staff dining-room, as was the custom at the Shelter. But he stayed and ate with us.

Mira pointed to the wall: A small lift came up and three children removed the serving plates. The lift went up and down again bringing up soup with noodles, meat with potatoes, boiled cabbage and baked apples for desert. I ate quickly, everything tasted wonderful.

Mira ate slowly, looking at Miss Steffa who sat across the table from us.

Suddenly she whispered to me, "She reminds me of Mother."

I was flabbergasted. "What?! Miss Steffa looks like our mom?"

We had no photograph of our mother, and even if Mira described her a million times I still couldn't picture her.

"No," said Mira. "Mother was beautiful."

"Was Mother as tall as she?"

"No."

"So how come she reminds you of her?"

"I don't know."

"So why did you say that in the first place?!" I was upset with Mira.

But she suddenly looked like a little girl about to burst into tears. She said she had to go home, but I knew she really wanted to stay, that she had no wish to go back to Staszek and her baby, even if he doesn't cry so much anymore.

5

Josek announced that he would be my personal guard and that he would watch over me for the next three months. When I asked what he expected in exchange he just chuckled. He was three years older than me and two heads taller. He had broad shoulders, a square chin and a lopsided smile.

I left the question of payment for his services to be discussed later when we were alone. I didn't mention the matter when Miss Steffa was nearby. Josek arrived just when she had finished showing me the study halls, the laundry, the kitchen, the bathrooms, the toilets and the dormitory. Every now and then she stopped and waited for me to catch up with her, but not for a moment did she stop talking. "Your number is 33. You must hang your towel on hook number 33, together with the case for your toothbrush and toothpaste. When you finish the tube of toothpaste you'll get a new one. This is where you polish your shoes," and so on.

We arrived at the boys' dormitory. There were at least 50 beds there, and as Mira had said, they were covered with white sheets drawn tight showing absolutely no creases. There were thick warm blankets on every bed, and next to each bed, there was a small table. Miss Steffa arranged the folded clothes I had received on the shelves, and then she took a string with a small key out of her apron pocket."That's for the drawer," she said, handing me the key and opening a drawer in the bedside table – it was mine from now on.

"What am I supposed to put in there?" I asked.

"Whatever you like," she replied. "Photographs, things you collect, letters, money. Things like that."

That's not the kind of information you should give a thief. I was almost sorry to get a drawer where I could hide things stolen from other drawers. If there had been private drawers like this in the Shelter, they would have been the perfect hiding place for penknives and switch blades. Those were the most wanted items there. Everyone wished to acquire, find, steal, sell or hide them.

After that Josek informed me that he would be my protector for the next three months. I didn't react. Miss Steffa walked towards the door, reminding me to report to the boys' shower room in 15 minutes. There the Doctor would examine me, weigh and measure me and, most important, cut my curls short. By that time I already knew why they shaved children's heads in orphanages; it was because of the lice. But I did not want to think such itchy thoughts, which lead to other itchy thoughts about fleas and bedbugs and other insects that nip and bite, especially at night when one tries to sleep. I wanted to deal with this business of Josek.

I knew the rules of the street and the Shelter. On the street, one almost always pays money. For example, if some hoodlums take over a sidewalk or alley, they demand a fee to allow one through the area they have seized. Anyone who doesn't want to pay is beaten up or has to choose another route, or both. I usually managed to avoid paying because I could run through the streets without being caught.

In the Shelter I learnt that food – especially bread or fruit – or sometimes soap, or a blanket, or a coat, or some cigarettes, could serve as *protection dues* for hoodlums. New kids at the Shelter were always forced to pay protection dues so that they wouldn't get beaten up or robbed; or so that they could eat their food or use the showers. At the Shelter there was a big 15-year-old boy who forced a little boy to stroke his head every night till he fell asleep. I was sure that one day the little boy would do something terrible to the big boy after he had fallen asleep, but for as long as I was there nothing happened. The little boy did as he was told. He had to survive there, that's all.

"What's so funny?" I asked Josek after Miss Steffa left the room.

"Nothing," he replied, and he wiped the lopsided smile off his face.

As Josek had told me he would take care of me for three months, I gathered he wanted a monthly fee, multiplied by three, paid now and in advance. I looked him straight in the face and said, with a gruff voice, "I have no money to pay protection, and there is nothing I can do about it."

He said that he'd heard about protection fees and things like that, but that he didn't believe they existed anywhere near here. "Anyway," he concluded, "it doesn't work like that here."

"So how does it work?" I said with contempt.

"Probably the opposite of what you're familiar with. Every new boy gets a protector, a sort of mentor, who is responsible for him. You're lucky you got me...." He was so pleased with himself. "I will introduce you to people, show you the ropes, and every morning, noon and evening you will be with me, except for the time I am with my girlfriend. Then you keep your distance. Understood?" He smiled his lopsided smile again, but I did not smile back.

"For example, if I'm on duty in the kitchen, you join me and learn what has to be done in the kitchen. If I'm on cleaning duty, you learn how to clean. If I go to a children's committee meeting or if I'm chosen to serve as a judge in court, you sit next to me and listen. That way you learn the rules and regulations of this place. After three months I am sure you will be able to continue without my help. Is that clear?"

"I still don't know what you get in exchange," I said.

"I get nothing in exchange, neither from you nor from anyone else."

"So why should you go into all that trouble?" I tried to understand. "You don't even know me."

He said the idea had never crossed his mind. He had been at the orphanage since he was seven years old, and this whole business of mutual help had made sense to him from the start.

"What are you – a saint?" I asked, smiling to myself. My grandma used to say of people like him, that with such an air of superiority he would soon piss olive oil! She used to like these sayings in *Yiddish*. Mira thought that Grandma invented some of them just to reinforce her arguments or to amuse herself.

Josek was disappointed by my cynicism.

"Here the seniors help the juniors, and when they themselves become seniors, they will help those who come after them." He understood that I didn't buy all his nonsense. "Just think of me as an older brother."

"Thanks, but I already have a sister," I replied sourly.

"There's only one thing..." he added, and I thought to myself, here it comes; now he's going to ask for something in return for all the caretaking and guarding. But he asked for nothing; he just explained. "If you do something wrong, like beat someone up, or make a mess or steal, I am responsible."

"What does that mean?" I asked and clenched my hand over the key that Miss Steffa had given me.

"Look, you need my help. But you have to behave yourself so that I'll want to help you. I don't have to be your mentor if I don't want to, if you don't deserve it, or if I suffer from it. Get it?"

Only now did I begin to understand what he meant by this arrangement.

"Do you know the saying, *Man is wolf to man*?"

"Yes, I do," I replied, even though I wasn't sure.

"Well, here it's not like that. Here man is friend to man, not wolf."

I wondered whether he knew that my surname was *Wolf*.

6

I had eaten, and I was tired and clean. My shaved head rested on a soft pillow and my body was covered by a warm blanket. I should have been able to fall asleep but I wasn't. I just lay there – one boy awake out of 50 – and felt so strange and different; I didn't belong.

Of course, I had Josek, but he made me nervous. All the time he was showing off how superior he was to me. Not even a day had gone by and I already knew that he was a member of the student council; that he was on a committee for instructive and at the same time amusing games, and that he belonged to all kinds of other committees and councils, all of them very important and useful. He also played volleyball, was a member of a Zionist youth movement. He even knew some Hebrew. And he was tall and broad-shouldered and considered handsome. He had a girlfriend. How could I not be uptight having someone like him around?

I thought to myself: I've managed to get through the first day without anyone threatening me, scolding me, bulling me or trying to hit me. This is nothing like the *Shelter*. The food, the bed, the sheets, the Doctor, Miss Steffa, Josek, the bathroom – everything is so different, and so much nicer. In a few days, few weeks at most, I'll get used to everything and be just like everybody else.

That's not true, whispered a small cruel voice inside me. You'll never be one of them. You've seen them. They are like one big family, and you are a lone wolf. You don't fit in.

- Why? What doesn't fit? They are all orphans, and at one time or another they must have felt as I am feeling now.
- Yes, but they all came here when they were still little, before they could be damaged. Staszek was right: The Street has ruined you.
- Staszek is a moron!
- The main thing is: Let's see you stop stealing.
- I can't run, remember?
- So you won't grab and run. You'll find another way. In the end you are what you are, a thief and a son of a thief.
- Shut up!

A few seconds passed quietly and then it all began again:

- You should have seen how stupid you looked in that bathroom.
- That was the first time I ever had a bath. And in a porcelain tub. Up till now I always washed myself standing in a wash tub, using water I heated on the stove, and suddenly I could sit down, almost lie down in the bath tub, with the water coming out of the wall, one tap for hot water and the other for cold. It was so strange in the beginning.
- Just leave me alone!
- What do you want from me?

Luckily someone started crying – one of the younger kids – and put an end to the upsetting dialogue between me and myself. It was a quiet sobbing, not nerve-racking screams like Shmulik's. It probably didn't disturb anyone, because no one got up to calm him down or shout at him.

A few minutes later the Doctor walked in and went quietly to the crying boy. I turned towards the sound as if in my sleep and saw the

23

Doctor bend over and whisper something. The boy threw his arms around the Doctor's neck and hugged him. They stayed like that for a few moments till the boy calmed down and lay back in bed. The Doctor put the blanket over him, kissed his forehead and stood waiting until the little boy was completely calm. Then he walked through the dormitory, stopping at every single bed, here and there arranging a blanket, sometimes lingering for a moment until he finally came to my bed. I closed my eyes, pretending to be asleep. But my eyes must have moved under my eyelids because he realized that I was awake.

"Janek, can't you fall asleep?" he whispered.

I sat up and smiled, a bit embarrassed.

He sat down on the edge of my bed.

I didn't know what to say so I asked, "You go from bed to bed to see who can't sleep?"

He chuckled quietly.

Maybe my questions are idiotic, I thought, because they seem to make everyone laugh, first Josek and now the Doctor.

"I am a children's doctor," he explained, "and this is just another way of examining each child. As I pass by the beds, I listen to the children's breathing. Breath sounds: wheezing, rasping, bubbly or frothy sounds; rapid breathing or snoring all may indicate some problem in the nose, throat or lungs."

Now it seemed to me that I could hear not only my own breathing but also that of all the other boys in the room. Suddenly I had an idea. Why didn't I think of it before? After all I did know that he was a doctor.

"Can you repair my limp leg?" I asked.

This time he did not think my question was funny. He answered in all seriousness, "I don't know if that's possible."

Earlier, when he weighed and measured me, he had also looked at my legs, especially at the one I dragged, the one that hurt. He examined the huge scar under my knee. Now he said, "If you wish, I can take you to the hospital to have your leg examined. Would you like that?"

I nodded and lay back on the pillow.

"There is a way to examine the leg. It's actually like taking a photograph," he explained. "The camera sends rays right through to the bones. It's called an X-ray. And when you look at it you can see inside the body. It doesn't hurt at all. Would you like me to arrange that for you?"

I nodded, but this time with my eyes closed. I didn't want him to see that I was crying.

7

Josek woke me at 6.30 in the morning. Half asleep I got up and did what everybody else was doing – washed my face, brushed my teeth and put my toothbrush and toothpaste back in my case which I hung on hook number 33. I made my bed, folded my blanket and changed my clothes. Josek, who had already washed and dressed when he woke me, wrote something in his little notebook.

"Up to now, you are okay," he smiled his lopsided smile and I gathered that he was writing about me. I nodded, still half asleep.

We went downstairs and the first thing we had to do was to swallow a small cup of cod liver oil. "Pinch your nose when you pour this stuff down your throat," advised Josek as he drank it. He then took a piece of bread from a basket and chewed it quickly. "It helps a little to get rid of the awful taste." I did the same. The bread hardly helped, but I didn't mind because the doctor had explained that the oil strengthens the bones, and I hoped it would help mend my bad leg.

Then we walked down to the ground floor and stood in line in front of the small room, where I had first met Korczak. During the half hour before breakfast, the room turned into *The Little Shop*. Miss Steffa would hand out ink, pencils and notebooks. Josek suggested we ask for an extra notebook.

"What for?" I asked.

"Perhaps there are things you want to ask me and don't feel comfortable saying them out aloud," he explained slowly, like a teacher speaking to a slow child. "You can write down questions or thoughts and I can respond. What do you say?"

"I don't like it," I said. Why does he patronize me?

"What a pity," Josek was disappointed. "It helped me when I first came here. I wrote down all kinds of things I didn't have the courage to ask my guardian. Her written answers reassured me."

"I think it's more suitable for little children or for girls," I replied.

He remained silent.

"Perhaps rather than corresponding, just let me see what you have written about me," I said pointing to the notebook in his pocket.

"No," he answered sourly. "In this I write things I have to report about you."

Josek approached a friend of his who stood in line in front of us. This friend needed a new exercise book and gave Miss Steffa his old one. "Itcho, please try to take good care of it so you don't annoy your teacher," she said to him before handing him a new one.

For me she had a schoolbag, notebooks, a pen with a nib, an inkwell and two books. I took my new schoolbag and, limping, followed Josek to our table in the dining room. Jugs of cocoa, rolls, butter, jam and honey were laid out on the table. I drank some hot cocoa and only then did I fully wake up. Then it hit me! He didn't say it was impossible to fix my leg. He said he would take me to the hospital. They will X-ray the bones and it won't hurt. I got up to look for him but he wasn't there.

"Where is the Doctor?" I asked Josek.

"He isn't always here," he answered, taking a bite of his roll. "Perhaps he's gone to the other orphanage, perhaps to a conference or a consultation, to a house call, or maybe he's meeting with someone from the radio or from Palestine or from another country. You never know! He is the busiest person in the world!"

I had no idea what he was talking about. What other orphanage? How is the Doctor connected to the radio? What is the meaning of house calls, and what does he have to do with Palestine? But all this was of no interest to me at the time. The only thing that worried me was that he might disappear before keeping his promise.

"But he will be back today, won't he?" I asked.

"I have no idea. Eat."

I was hungry and Josek said I could take another roll and fill my cup again. "But if you take another helping you must finish everything on your plate, otherwise it's just a waste."

"Of course," I replied. I never left any food on my plate. At home I used to lick the plate after I finished eating so as not to waste a single crumb. Mira used to lick her plate too but asked me never to do so in front of other people.

The noise of cutlery and crockery clanging and mouths chewing fast filled the room. A young woman with a head full of curls ran towards our table and sat in one of the empty chairs. "Forgive me! This is terrible! I just cannot get here on time! Miss Steffa is right to scold me. *How can you ask the children to be on time when you yourself are always late?!*" she tried to imitate Miss Steffa's voice and her clipped way of speaking. Then she took a deep breath and in her regular voice said good morning to all the children, including me. She already knew my name.

Josek said, "She's forgotten to mention that her name is Hella and that she is a tutor."

"Pleased to meet you," Hella said while putting out her hand.

"Janek is my little brother for the next three months," Josek introduced me, and then, without looking at me, added, "Listen Janek, it's true that Hella is always late but that is her *only* fault."

"Josek you are such a flatterer." Hella laughed, and a few curls escaped from her messy bun. Josek was pleased with himself, as though he had been paid a compliment. I swallowed another bite of bread.

"This is why I have been chosen as a *fellow* ever since my first year here," boasted Josek and explained that each year the children of the orphanage cast a vote regarding every child. Everybody receives one of three designations: *Fellow*, *Resident* or *Indifferent resident*.

"Indifferent resident?" I asked drily.

"Someone who couldn't care less about anything, and usually the other children don't care for him either. Anyway, it is unusual for anyone to achieve the title *fellow* in his first year as I did." He looked at me as if he expected me to applaud.

"What are the benefits of being a *fellow*? I asked in an even drier tone.

"Janek is always interested in the benefits," Josek said smiling at Hella, and then looked at me.

"In addition to the honor, I also have special privileges."

"Such as?"

"For example, I am allowed to visit my family more often than others."

Wonderful! In any case I had no intention of visiting my family. And then he announced, "The vote concerning you will be held in a month."

"What do you mean? You said once a year!" Now he had me worried.

"True, but also after the first month. In the first vote there are three slips of paper: *Plus*, *Minus* and *Zero*. *Plus* means they like you, *Minus* means they can't stand you and *Zero* means they are indifferent. If most of your slips are minus, then you have a real problem".

"Even if I haven't broken any rules?" I asked.

"Yes," he replied. "Of course my report is also taken into consideration, but your situation won't be good if most of us are not happy to have you here. You will be on probation for a year." He talked as though this had already happened. Why does he need to put so much pressure on me? I took a deep breath. The Doctor won't want to bother with an X-ray at the hospital if he sees the children are not happy with me.

"He can't be gone for a long time, can he?"

"Who?"

"The Doctor."

Josek shrugged, wrote something in his damn notebook and got to his feet. I got up myself, but continued to look at the bread rolls on the table.

"May I take some to school?" I finally asked.

"You don't have to," he replied, "Come, have a look."

At the door Miss Steffa stood with two baskets on her arm, one with cheese rolls, the other with sausage rolls. I took my coat off hook number 33 and stood in line. Every child chose a roll and ran towards the gate. When my turn came I suddenly felt as if I was paralyzed. I couldn't move my hand. The boy behind me pushed me. "Go on, you have to choose a roll, not a bride. Come on, move it!"

I wanted to turn round and beat him up, but I just stood there and felt like an idiot. I wished I could run, but at that moment I couldn't even move.

"Janek, is everything okay?" Miss Steffa asked.

I remained silent. She took my schoolbag and quickly put two rolls in it, one of each kind.

"When will the Doctor come back?" I managed to mumble.

The boy behind me announced that he wanted a roll with sausage.

"In the evening," answered Miss Steffa, turning to him.

I relaxed. I walked down the steps towards the gate. I saw Josek standing next to a girl. Even from a distance I could see that she was beautiful. He waved to me to hurry up. The first lesson was to begin in exactly a quarter of an hour. Up till now I was too busy to think about going back there, to the same school, to study with children at least a year younger than me. Miss Steffa said the teacher told her that he remembered that I had been a good student. If not for that, they would have put me in a class two years below, as I had not been there for more than a year and a half. Never mind! I consoled myself and walked faster. What is more important is that the Doctor will be back tonight.

8

But of course Beautiful Rosie was Josek's girlfriend. On the way to school they only had eyes for each other, giggling and smiling, he with his lopsided smile and she with a sharpish one.

One day after school, when the children from the orphanage assembled in order to walk back together, Rosie talked to me, while Josek talked to Itcho – with great excitement and arm waving – about the upcoming soccer game. They argued who were the most suitable captains for each team. Had they known me before my injury they would have chosen me to be their team captain, for sure. Not only would they have wanted me, they would have begged! I was born to run! That was what I was thinking about when Beautiful Rosie asked me, "How was school today, after having been away for such a long time?"

"A little strange," I replied.

"Exciting?" she asked, adjusting the ribbon which held her straight brown hair in a low pony tail.

"I have to repeat a grade, although I don't think I missed much."

"That's good," she smiled. "And how do you feel with us?"

"I'm okay, I think."

"You're lucky to have Josek," she said with a warm tone in her voice.

She was tall and dark but her eyes were pale blue, almost transparent. There was something about her, not only her hair, but also her skin and face, that was smooth and soft.

"Josek wants to be an instructor in the youth movement. I keep telling him that when the time comes for him to leave he should ask to stay and instruct us. He is a born leader!"

It was clear that she was in love with him, and our conversation proceeded slowly, just like me, limping along by her side, but Rosie did not give up. "What do you want to be when you grow up?" she asked.

It was such a silly question that I felt like replying *A fireman.*

"There are some people you can tell what they'll become when they grow up, like Izchak, for example," she said, pointing at a boy in front of us. "He will be an artist, a great painter. He is lucky to have three great gifts: First, he has talent, second, he has the motivation to use his talent, and third, he has the opportunity to do what he is good at. Don't you think so?"

"Yes," I replied. "But most people don't have a great talent."

"And even if they do have a great talent," said Rosie, "most of them don't have the opportunity to discover and develop it. Poor people don't have the same opportunities as rich people." She didn't sound like a small child any more.

Josek turned around, smiled and shouted, "Careful, Janek, my girlfriend will soon turn you into a communist!"

"This has nothing to do with communism," Rosie said firmly. "Even though my brother is a communist and he taught me to see these things."

There were people, like Staszek for instance, for whom the word *communist* was a curse, and having a communist in the family was regarded a disgrace. But Rosie was not ashamed of her brother, nor of any member of her family.

"My mother," she told me one day on our way back from school, "worked as a peddler in the market ever since she was a little girl. She didn't know how to do anything else, she didn't even know how to read and write. She died when I was very young."

"So did my mother," I said.

Our eyes met for a moment.

"In any case," she turned away and went on with the previous subject, "nobody thought that she might have a special talent. That perhaps she could do something else besides standing in the market and calling out the price of a chicken. And even if someone had thought so, where would the money have come from to give her a chance? There is no such thing as equal rights. That's why the poor remain poor, and poor women suffer more than anyone else."

What she said confused me. I had read about such matters in the newspapers – poverty versus affluence, equal opportunity, the state of women compared to that of men – but no one had talked to me about them, certainly not a 12-year-old girl! My grandmother used to say about me, "That cucumber grew up pickled," meaning that I was not childlike enough for my age, that I was born an adult, serious and sour. Rosie too, I thought to myself, was born an adult, even more than me, but she did not seem sour at all. On the contrary, there was something lady-like about her. After all, her question – what do you want to do when you grow up? – didn't seem childish any more.

I asked her what she had planned for herself, and she answered decisively, "I hope I'll have enough money to study. My brother will help me. Even now he is saving up for me to go to law school. I want to be a lawyer."

"Ah, and then you'll make a lot of money."

"True, but it's not that simple. The university sets a limit on the number of women students, and also for the number of Jews there is a fixed quota. My brother, David, says I had better go to Paris or Moscow in order to study. Anyway, I'll always remember where I came from, and when I finish my studies I'll represent those underdogs, the weak, the poor, women."

I remained silent.

"What do you think?" she asked and threw me a challenging glance.

I was confused. Mira and I knew that we were poor, but we never talked about it in a general way, like Rosie and her brother. We talked about our own poverty, how would we manage to buy food, to pay rent, things like that. I was surprised by Rosie's idealism which seemed to be genuine and honest and didn't sound false like Josek's. Besides, I was sorry to hear that she might not be accepted at the University of Warsaw, especially because I didn't want her to go to Paris, as if that would happen next week. And another thing: She never mentioned poor children, only poor adults and especially women. Of all the things going through my head the only thing I could say was, "I think that poor children are the ones who need help the most."

A wide smile spread across her face. "You think like the Doctor. Everything he does, he does in order to help children, especially the poor ones. He believes there is hope for children and that it is worth fighting for us; so that we can have a good life now, and that we'll have a better future than our parents." She took a deep breath and added, "It is because of him and because of my brother that I am not selling chickens in the market."

I almost fainted. She, the Beautiful Rosie, had compared me, Janek Wolf, to the Doctor. I wanted to say something to impress her, something that would make up for my ugly limp. And I had something to say! I had once raised the spirits of all the people in the city; people had counted on me to win a gold medal! I was supposed to be Poland's champion runner, the next Janush Kusosinski! You say that Izchak is a gifted painter? I was once a gifted runner!

Fortunately I kept all those things to myself, and just said, "Up until a few months ago, I had planned to run the marathon, to compete in an international race, perhaps the Olympics. Do you understand? This limp is something recent, before that I could really run very fast."

Her eyes filled with pain. Oh God, that was not what I intended at all! I really didn't want her to pity me! So I added quickly, "Perhaps it's better this way! If I hadn't been injured I might not have discovered what I am really good at!"

As soon as the words were out of my mouth, I was sorry I had said them. In a moment she is going to ask me what I am really good at, where my real talent lies. So in order to prevent such a question, I started chattering away, "You understand, you cannot work on anything else when you're training, professionally I mean, for a race, like for the Olympic Games. You have to be dedicated to it. Everything else then is just background noise...." etc., blah blah blah...

Luckily, Josek arrived and put his arm round her shoulders. Finally I could stop rattling away, and my unrevealed talent was left floating in the air like a great promise. Beautiful Rosie didn't ask about it. In fact, we didn't talk again until after lunch. I sat quietly in the room next to the great hall. This room was reserved for quiet tasks like doing homework, saying prayer. Sometimes, important meetings were held there. Now I was immersed in my homework and didn't notice that Beautiful Rosie had walked in and come up to my table. Suddenly the words "There is a message for you," were breathed into my ear and made me jump. I almost fell off my chair. Rosie laughed. "Sorry, sorry, sorry," she said smiling her lovely smile. "How can you concentrate in this noise?" I raised my head. Indeed three boys were involved in a raucous argument and the instructor who was there to help with homework did his best to hush them up. From the adjacent hall music could be heard, a piano, a trumpet and perhaps a mandolin were playing. But I had heard nothing of all that. I have this gift: if I'm doing anything, like reading, doing my homework, listening to music or running, I am completely immersed in it. Mira used to say, "The world can fall to pieces, and he won't even sneeze!"

A little girl from the second grade who looked in despair at the book and notebook in front of her asked Rosie for help. Beautiful Rosie went over to her and I limped over to the notice board in the great hall to find the message left for me. I scanned the notes. There was the list for kitchen duty, a summons for a trial: Leah has lodged a complaint against Abraham for spitting at her (how disgusting!). Abraham writes in his defense that she insulted him and that he did not spit at her but in her direction. There was another notice about a trial – someone had lent someone else a toy or game which was never returned. The defendant gave a list of excuses: I lost it, I forgot it, I lent it to someone else, etc. There was also a curious list of pairs of children who made appointments to beat each other up, and next to it another list of cancellations of the dates for beating each other up.

Someone wrote that she had lost a heart-shaped locket asking the finder to please return it. At the bottom right-hand corner of the board I found a short notice: "Janek, the nearest appointment available for an X-ray is Wednesday, three weeks from today. I booked it for you, and will, of course, accompany you. Signed: Korczak."

"Something good?" I heard Beautiful Rosie's incisive voice behind me.

I turned around with a flourish. "The best!"

I was so happy that I felt I could kiss her and even Josek, who was standing next to her.

"I am on laundry duty," he said. "Coming?"

"Yes," I replied and thought to myself that I wished I could steal his girlfriend.

9

Time flew by as the day of my approached. My nerves were on edge, so much that I almost forgot about Mira and how mad I was at her. All I wanted was that my probation period would pass without a hitch, so I did all I could to show my best behavior. School was pretty hard. I had missed so much material and had almost forgotten how to study. After school, at the orphanage, I prepared my homework diligently and did all that was expected of me. But I knew that it was not enough to insure that the others would not give me a *zero*. I didn't know how to be friendly, couldn't strike up a conversation easily, like Beautiful Rosie, and I didn't offer anyone any help. I wasn't amiable, like Josek, nor was I a leader. I am serious and withdrawn. In the past that didn't worry me, because I was good at sports but I could no longer count on that.

I was also worried about how Josek would evaluate me. I felt like stealing his notebook to find out what he really thought of me, especially to know what his reply would be when the Doctor asked him for his opinion about his trainee. Two scenarios ran through my head: if Josek had written in his notebook that I was praiseworthy, I would just return it and calm down. But if the notebook was full of complaints on why I should be there, I would tear out those pages or just throw it down the drain! Josek may look for it in the sewer.

I remembered of course that the Doctor mentioned during our very first meeting, that the children's court can expel one for stealing. But this wouldn't be stealing; I tried to convince myself that it would help me find my faults. And besides, I had no wish to steal the notebook, just to read what was written in it.

I did it on Friday, after finishing the preparations for Sabbath. As in the previous week we were divided into five groups of ten boys, and each group took its turn in the bathroom. I was in the last group. We started in the shoe corner. As in the previous week the Doctor polished his shoes together with us, and we all brushed away with fervor. When the shoes were done, he sent us to bathe. I waited for everyone to leave and then I asked the Doctor, "We're going to the X-ray on Wednesday, aren't we?"

He raised his head and looked at me with his kind eyes. "Yes, after lunch."

I stayed for another moment. He lifted a shoe, looked at it and then lifted another. He wrote something down in his little notebook, and then lifted another shoe. It looked like he was giving marks for shoe polishing. "Did you write in your notebook that I'm an expert shoe-polisher or that I'm a rotten one?" I asked.

"Oh, I'm sorry. I had no idea that this is what it looks like," he replied, surprised. "I am looking at the shoes to see who needs a new pair. Perhaps someone has outgrown his shoes or perhaps the shoes are worn. I can also see if a problem is developing in someone's foot from the imprint of his foot inside the shoe, or from uneven wearing of the sole."

"But why are you writing it down in your notebook?"

"When you write something down you can see if a problem arises over time. It also helps me remember. For example," he said, waving a shoe with a completely worn sole, "I have to tell Miss Steffa that Mark needs a new pair of shoes again."

Afterwards we had our bath, and everyone was measured and weighed by the Doctor. Between one child and the next he added something to his notes.

And then, just like on the previous Friday, he cut our nails. "As far as I know you," he said while cutting my thumbnail with his tiny scissors, "you already know why I am doing this, don't you?"

I wanted to answer correctly, not like the first night when I thought he was checking who was awake when he was actually listening to our breathing, or like 15 minutes ago when I thought he was grading us on how we polished our shoes when he was actually checking our feet and shoes.

"Something connected with our health?" I asked hesitantly. A smile spread across his face up toward his bald patch. I was right! I had once read an article all about fingernails. It said that the thickness and color of the nails can indicate health problems, and that people who bit their nails to the bone, like Mira, were terribly nervous even if they looked quiet and peaceful.

"Perhaps you can discover all sorts of diseases from the thickness and color of the nails, or just discover who is nervous and who isn't," I replied with confidence.

He lifted his head. "You are absolutely right, Janek!"

"I once read an article in a newspaper on fingernails," I admitted.

"There is another reason, though," he said.

"Please tell me." He was about to finish with me, and I still had no idea why he cut everybody's nails by himself, once a week.

"I am very busy," he explained. "I regret I haven't got the time to spend more time with each child one-on-one. This is my opportunity to speak with each of you privately. A child can tell me what is bothering him, and I can also talk with him and tell him what is bothering us about him."

"I understand."

"For instance, now I want to talk to you about something which is bothering me."

He had reached the last fingernail.

"The X-ray on Wednesday will show us what cannot be seen with the naked eye. You have an inquisitive mind and wish to understand things fully, and that is exactly what this examination makes possible."

It was pleasant to hear that this was the impression he had of me. I had no idea I was like that.

"After looking at the X-ray," he continued. "We'll know what we can do to help. Remember this is just an examination, not a treatment. Meaning that as far as your limp or your pain is concerned, you'll come out of there just as you went in. If you expect anything else you'll be terribly disappointed. Okay?"

I nodded.

He stroked my head with his warm hand and indicated that I should let my seat for the next boy.

When I was all clean and dressed up in my best clothes the gong sounded for the Friday night meal which was the most important, festive and tastiest meal of the week. Most of the children were already seated at the tables in the hall, and those who weren't were running down the stairs. I don't know how the idea came to me, but I suddenly knew where Josek kept his little notebook: in the drawer of his nightstand. So instead of joining the other children I made my way straight there. I opened the drawer easily with my special key. There were some interesting items there – postcards and letters, perhaps from Beautiful Rosie, a few photographs and some money; but I had no time to rummage: I just took the notebook, sat on the floor and started leafing through it. There was a tardiness chart, table of late arrivals, Josek noted that at least three times I had stayed in bed too long or dallied in the bathroom and made him late. There was also a graph showing I was adjusting to the orphanage, my cleanliness and neatness marks remained stubbornly low.

Josek had written some remarks under the heading "Thoughts and observations concerning Janek": "hostile but not violent, always afraid he'll be asked to do something, not easy to like, a hard nut to crack." At the bottom of one page I saw a remark: "Up to now does not excel at anything or shows any special talent." On another page appeared this remark: "Suffers from an inferiority complex, probably because he is lame. All sorts of rumors are circulating: Some say he was beaten up at another orphanage because he was the only Jew there, others say he stole jewels from an old woman and tried to escape by climbing out of the window and fell. I also heard that he was always like that, because his mother dropped him when he was a baby and that she did it on purpose. If this is true, no wonder he doesn't trust anyone."

I got up from the floor and put the notebook back in the drawer – what was the point of throwing it away? – and went downstairs. Everybody was already seated. The smell of fresh *Challa* bread was in the air, the candles were lit and the beginning of a Sabbath melody could be heard. But none of the festive feeling touched me. In my heart it was snowing, as my Grandma used to say. Miss Steffa looked at me as I took my seat next to Josek. Why did she remind Mira of our mother, I wondered, and a wave of heat rose from my collar toward my ears. Josek's comment about my mother hurt the most! How could they say such a thing? True, I didn't know her, but one thing I knew for sure: she would have never, never throw me, her baby, to the floor.

10

After breakfast on Saturday morning we took our chairs from the dining hall to the quiet room where, exactly at ten o'clock, the Doctor began reading out aloud from the orphanage weekly. This was our very own newspaper, very different from the ones I had stolen on the street. The news items were written like those in a daily newspaper but reported only things that had happened at the orphanage or were about to happen. There was also an editorial written by Korczak himself. In it, he requested the children to write to the paper not only about what had happened to them at school or at the orphanage, but also about matters concerning their families so that we would know whether any help was needed, if anyone was in trouble, or if anyone had a celebration he could share with us, like the birth of a new baby.

That's all I need, I thought, that Mira should have another baby. The Doctor read aloud letters sent to the editor and a short story written by Beautiful Rosie, about a girl from a poor family who worked as a servant during the day and studied at night.

I wasn't really listening, because I was thinking of something I would like to write and send to the newspaper to be read aloud next Saturday. The heading would be *You don't know me*. I would write that my mother did not drop me on the floor, not on purpose and not by accident. I wanted to write that she cradled me in her arms all the time, and that she loved to rest her cheek on my head in order to calm me, just the way Mira does with Shmulik. But then I realized I remembered nothing of the time Mother and I were together, before she died. I had no idea whether she had enough strength to carry me around or whether she was so sick that she lay in bed all day. Perhaps they were afraid I would catch her disease, which is why they kept me away from her. I really had no idea. I thought that I should ask Mira, but then I drove that thought away. Saturday was visiting day, and most children spent the afternoon with their families, but not me. I knew that Mira was waiting. She knew that on Saturday children visited their families. Let her wait! After what had happened to me at the Shelter, after she abandoned me here – I was done with her!

In my letter to the newspaper I planned to point out that I had never broken into a house. Breaking into somebody's house seemed to me far worse than just grabbing something in the street. I wanted to stress the fact that I never stole from old people, but that was not entirely true. At least once I had stole a newspaper from an old man, and another time I stole a cake from an old lady as she came out of a pastry shop. But I tried to do it gently. I didn't push her. I respect old people, mainly because of my grandmother, who used to complain about aches and pains and other trouble that come with old age. She used to say that people are born soft and smooth and as the years go by they become harder and courser, but not forever. When they grow really old they become soft again, even fragile; and that is why they should be handled gently, otherwise they'll crumble.

To get back to what I was planning to write: I didn't mean to refer to why I was beaten up at the previous orphanage. I hoped that they would think that it was because I was a Jew and not because I was a thief. I did want to respond to what Josek had written about me not having any talent, but what could I write? That I was once a champion athlete?

After the Doctor finished reading the newspaper, five boys and Miss Steffa walked into the quiet room. They were the judges for the trials of that week. They had just returned from their weekly meeting in court and took their seats opposite us at the table covered with a green baize cloth. Miss Steffa, who acted as the court clerk, began reading the complaints and each judge was requested to voice his opinion.

Suddenly I realized that I would have a problem with the defense I was preparing for publication in the newspaper, because then Josek would know I had peeped into his journal. Let him know! I said to myself. He has no proof!

Since I had read his diary I had hardly talked to him. Now when he asked me whether I intended to go home for the weekend, I just shrugged. He invited me, his *hard nut to crack*, to join him, Beautiful Rosie and her big brother at the cinema. He even suggested that before the film, I should come with him to visit his family. "No thank you," I replied coldly.

The Doctor also noticed I had no intention of leaving. "This Saturday you may go home. A large group of children is leaving by tram in the direction of your home. Hella the tutor is going with them. Do you wish to join them and visit your sister?

"No, thank you, not this Saturday," I tried to sound as if it was only this week that I did not want to visit my sister. I did not want him to put pressure on me to go.

"Today I prefer to stay here," I said, smiling.

The Doctor remained silent for a moment and then asked, "Do you want some newspapers?"

I smiled. He remembered from our first conversation that we both liked newspapers; and it was Saturday, the day the newspapers were thick. They had extra sections, the weekend editions, with a lot of interesting things to read, much more than in the thin daily editions. The Doctor brought me two Polish newspapers and promised to try and bring me a Yiddish newspaper. He himself, he said with some embarrassment, couldn't read or write Yiddish, he couldn't even speak the language. Nor did he know any Hebrew.

"I don't know any Hebrew either," I said.

"There is a Hebrew class here," he added before he left. "If you wish, you may join."

"We'll see," I said, just in order to be polite. I didn't think I wanted to.

I knew the Hebrew letters because when I was about four or five years old, Mira had sent me to study with other little Jewish boys in the cheder in our neighborhood. I was there only for a short while, perhaps a fortnight, because after the Rabbi had pulled my ears real hard, I refused to go back.

Now I sat in the quiet room reading the newspapers. This was the first time I read newspapers which had not been stolen.

"Can I have a section?" asked Itcho, who had pulled a chair over and sat next to me.

"What would you like? News, sports, culture, general interests," I asked.

"Something you don't need," he replied.

Itcho was the same age as I and we were in the same class. He had also been set back a year. He was short and sturdy, looked like a wrestler, and was hot tempered. But he was also funny and an excellent mimic. At school he was often punished and slapped on the palms of his hands with a ruler because of his antics and also because of his spelling mistakes. When that happened he acted as though he didn't care, smiled and even laughed occasionally.

I gave him the obituaries. Itcho looked at the black squares and the names of the departed and asked:

"What is this for?"

"To let people know who died."

"It isn't nice to make an airplane out of the dead," he said, while folding a sheet of newspaper with his fat and nimble fingers. He folded the paper again and again till it turned into a rose.

"Nice, isn't it?" he smiled proudly.

"Wonderful," I admitted.

"If you were a girl and were given this flower, you would never guess that I made it, right?"

"Even as a boy I wouldn't guess."

He seemed pleased with my reply. He wanted to leave the flower on some girl's bed – he didn't tell me whose – and was too shy to let her know it was from him.

"I am not at her level," he said sadly and then asked, "Can you keep a secret? If you're asked if you know who made this flower, don't say *Itcho made it*. Don't give me away."

"Don't worry; your secret is safe with me. I won't betray you even under torture."

He began a pantomime act, pulling on his fingers, twisting them, beating them with an imaginary hammer, and contorting his face as if in intense pain. He was really funny. Then he went upstairs to the girls' dormitory to put the flower on the girl's bed. I waited for him to return and then we went down to the kitchen to work with the other children who had not gone home.

We sat opposite each other on two small stools, peeling potatoes, and I told him why I was lame. He never mentioned the rumors, perhaps he hadn't heard them. He grabbed a potato and stabbed it.

"This is what the headmaster of that orphanage of yours deserves," he said and began peeling the potato quickly and energetically. Through pursed lips he made small whimpering sounds, as though the headmaster was begging him to stop peeling his skin. I laughed and laughed till everyone stared at Itcho and me.

"I'm not doing anything," Itcho shrugged his shoulders and continued poking and peeling his potatoes. I couldn't stop laughing. Tears streamed down my cheeks. The dreadful feeling I carried with me since I'd read Josek's notebook gradually subsided. I felt the ice melting in my heart. It became a puddle.

11

_____

I put Korczak's note into my empty private drawer, but by that time everyone had read the note and knew that I was about to go to the hospital. As the day came nearer, more and more children asked me what an X-ray was, what happens during the examination, how long it would take and would it hurt? I answered as best I could, which wasn't much, just what the Doctor had told me. Some children, not just the little ones, asked me to tell them all about it when I got back. They were fascinated by the fact that the rays could penetrate right to the bone without cutting it or causing pain.

When I got back from school on the day of the examination Josek asked me whether I would be X-rayed at the hospital in Szliska Street.

"I don't know," I replied. "Why?"

"The Doctor used to work there, before he and Miss Steffa opened the orphanage."

And Itcho added mischievously, "Before they threw him out!"

"What? The Doctor was fired!?"

"That's what they say," Beautiful Rosie joined the conversation. She was walking arm-in-arm with her best friend, Hannah, and they looked like exact opposites. Rosie was dark-skinned and slim, and Hannah fair and round, like the white rolls we had for breakfast.

"Did you ever consider that it's just a rumor?" I asked while I tried

47

not to lose my temper. I wanted to add that soon they would say that the doctor had dropped a baby on the floor on purpose and that was why he was fired.

Itcho looked at me and said, "We are not saying anything bad about him!"

I kept my mouth shut.

"On the contrary," said Hannah and Rosie added, "Josek knows the story well. Josek, would you tell him about Aharon?"

Josek was reluctant. Aharon, his father's younger brother and his favorite uncle, had died a year earlier. It seemed he didn't want to be reminded of him. His eyes grew misty as soon as his uncle's name was mentioned. Rosie suggested she would start with the background and Josek ought to continue. He nodded and she began by telling me that the Doctor's real name was not Janusz Korczak at all. It was Henryk Goldszmit. He had signed the first story he had written as Janusz Korczak and after it was published he stuck to the name. She said it was his pseudonym, and then asked if I had read his book, *When I Shall Be Small Again*. I hadn't read it.

"And you, Itcho?" she asked

"Well, what do you think?!" was his answer. For him reading was torture.

Hannah said, "I think it's his best book because he tells the story from the point of view of a 10-year-old boy and of an adult at the very same time."

Itcho stopped her. "Thanks, but the library is closed now. Josek, tell us the story of your uncle and save us from a lesson in literature."

Hannah's feelings were clearly hurt but she said nothing. Josek began his story. When Aharon, his beloved uncle, was four years old, he suddenly became very ill. His mother, Josek's grandmother, was afraid to take her little boy to the hospital because she knew that visitors were only allowed once a week and then only for a very short while, and only two at a time. She knew that little Aharon would be sad and lonely in the hospital without his mother or anyone he knew. In the end, she had no choice because he got even sicker. Aharon stayed at the hospital for a long time, for months perhaps, he hated the doctors and the nurses, the painful examinations and treatments, the terrible medications and the smell of the place. He waited for visiting day, when his mother would bring along one of his brothers, hopefully Josek's father. He knew that the rest of the family would be waiting outside; hoping that perhaps one of them would be allowed to enter the hospital and say a brief hello to the little boy.

Josek said that his uncle remembered the day the Doctor arrived at the hospital because after that everything had changed, for the better of course. When Dr. Goldszmit examined patients, it never hurt, in contrast to all the other doctors. He never used force, was careful with injections and was very patient. The children loved him because he joked with them, told stories and even doled out sweets. He asked them how they were as though he was really interested. And they gave him truthful answers. They told him not only about their aches and pains but also how much they missed their families. Because only weekly visits were allowed, they felt they were being treated like criminals in prison, and not like sick children in hospital.

The Doctor sided with the children and even made an agreement with them. If they would take their medicine as ordered, without cheating by pouring part of it on the floor, for example, or by keeping the pill under their tongues and then spitting them out, he would allow all the visitors waiting outside to come in. Both sides kept their part of the agreement, and for some weeks visiting days were like one big party.

"Why do they limit visits in hospitals?" I asked.

"So that the children don't catch more diseases from the visitors, and that the visitors don't catch diseases from the sick children," answered Hannah in her deep voice.

"Why are you interrupting?" Itcho fumed, and Josek went on. "The children felt better because they now took their medicine, and their mood improved because they got to see their families."

Josek turned to me. "If you were the director of the hospital wouldn't you have been pleased with the Doctor?"

"Sure," I replied.

"Well, he wasn't!"

"No-one was pleased, except the children," added Rosie.

"And that's why they fired him?" I was astounded.

49

"Well, they watched him closely, and then the episode with my uncle occurred."

"The doctor was fired because of your uncle?!"

"Aharon is not to blame," Rosie stood up for him. "The doctor could have continued working in a private clinic and made a fortune, if he had asked for money instead of giving it away. But he was never interested in money."

"One could say that Aharon helped the Doctor to find his way to us," said Hannah.

"So be grateful that we don't have a director like the monster at the Shelter," added Itcho.

"The Doctor probably stopped working at the hospital without any connection to what happened with Aharon," said Josek. "War broke out and he was recruited to treat the wounded."

Itcho wouldn't relent. He said, "So tell us what happened with your uncle."

Josek said that Aharon hid part of his collection of small stones under his mattress, stones like the ones found in backyards. He liked to play with them. One day when one of the nurses changed the sheets, she found the stones and threw them out. When Aharon discovered that his collection was gone, he just cried and cried for hours. When the Doctor heard what had happened he called in the nurse and asked if she had indeed thrown away Aharon's collection.

At this point Itcho put his hands on his hips and started shouting as if he was the nurse at the hospital.

"What did you expect me to do, Dr. Goldszmit? The hospital is a sterile place! You call it *collection*? Let me tell you what it really was. Stones! Filthy stones from the streets, from boulders, from hills! And this cheeky boy, instead of thanking me, complains that I cleaned his bed!"

Itcho's performance made everybody laugh, except Josek. His square face remained serious. He continued his story and told us that Aharon always remembered how angry the Doctor had been and what he had said to the nurse: "How would you feel if someone threw away your jewelry?"

The nurse couldn't believe that the Doctor was comparing the precious stones in her earrings and necklaces to Aharon's dirty stones, and to make matters worse, the Doctor was now reprimanding her! In front of the children, when all she had done was what she thought was her duty. She was furious, and immediately went to see the director. A short while later the Doctor stopped working there, perhaps because they couldn't deal with his good heart or because of the war.

"So what do you think of the Doctor?" asked Itcho.

"He's a king," I replied.

"Like King Matt the First," added Hannah. "Janek, do you know the Doctor's book with that title?"

"You and your books again!" Itcho said angrily.

Josek told us that Uncle Aharon was glad for him when he was accepted into the orphanage. The whole family pitied him, but Aharon said that pity was completely misplaced, because Josek was lucky, like someone who found a fortune or won the lottery, or even better!

Suddenly, Josek announced that he would be accompanying me to the hospital.

"No!" I called out. "There's no need."

"What do you mean by 'there's no need?'" he said firmly. "I am responsible for you. Of course I'm coming with you! We'll have a fine day. Just you, the Doctor and me."

What a disaster! I felt my whole body grow cold. All the time I had thought that there would only be the two of us, the Doctor and me; that I would have him to myself, and now Josek had to interfere. I didn't know how to get rid of him.

When we entered the big hall a surprising way-out presented itself. A tall dark boy, about Josek's age, who went to vocational school and was nicknamed The *Photographer*, was waiting for us. He said, "The Doctor agreed that I accompany you to the hospital instead of Josek, but only if it's okay with both of you. What do you say?"

Before Josek could answer, the Photographer promised, "I won't disturb you, I just want to see how the X-ray machine works."

Beautiful Rosie looked at me beseechingly. She wanted Josek to stay with her.

"Fine by me," I replied.

"Thanks!" The Photographer's face lit up, Rosie and Josek smiled at each other. I realized that Josek really wanted to stay. It was his sense of duty that had made him offer to come with us.

"Are you sure?" he asked me.

"Sure, sure," I replied. I hardly knew the Photographer, but at that time I felt that anyone was better than Josek.

12

The next day, the three of us, the Doctor, the Photographer and I, took the tram to the hospital.

The Photographer told us that he rarely took the tram, not even on Saturdays when he visited his family. Mostly, he walked and sometimes, especially when it was very cold, he would run the whole way. I was jealous; it had been a long time since I had run anywhere. He explained that he was saving the fare money he received for the tram.

"I would never ride the tram without paying," he declared with a broad smile. His two front teeth were enormous and looked as strong as a cement wall.

"That was a long time ago," the Doctor said sheepishly.

"We had to go to court," the Photographer told me gleefully. "The Doctor jumped on a moving tram."

"You're joking!" I said.

"I swear!" said the Photographer.

The Doctor explained, "I am human, I also make mistakes, but I gave my word to the court that I would never do it again, and I stuck to my promise. It is indeed stupid to jump on a moving tram, not only because it is wrong to steal a ride but also because it is dangerous."

I noticed he said *to steal*.

"My Aunt Mina's brother-in-law jumped on a moving tram and fell under it. They had to cut off his leg," said the Photographer, and then he pressed his face to the window.

"Look, look," he got all excited and tapped his finger on the window pane. "Did you see?"

"Who?" asked the Doctor.

"Retina."

It turned out that Retina was a camera displayed in a shop-window we happened to pass. Even if we had been able to look into the window packed with cameras we would not have been able to recognize his Retina. But for the Photographer that camera stood out amongst all the others. He talked about it as if it was a girl he was in love with. He explained that it was because of the camera that he did not take the tram on Saturdays. He had already saved up 10 Zloty, and until he had the whole sum needed to purchase the camera – about 300 Zloty – he would only be able to look at it through the shop window. The shopkeeper already knew him and once even allowed him to hold the camera. The Doctor began humming a famous love song and the Photographer smiled his buck-tooth smile.

When we got off the tram at the station near the hospital, the Doctor turned to me and said, "Remember, this is only an examination."

"Of course," I replied.

Still, I was very excited, as if I was going in for an operation or something like that. The hospital was huge. We walked along lengthy corridors, down some stairs on one side and up some stairs on the other. My lame leg hurt even more than usual, perhaps just because of the thought that soon the X-rays would penetrate it. Finally we arrived at a large and rather dark waiting room with benches along the walls. Right at the end, a nurse in a white coat was sitting at a desk near a bookshelf full of paper files. When she saw the Doctor she rose from her chair and stretched out her hand.

"Welcome, Doctor Goldszmit. How are you Doctor Goldszmit?" and "The professor is waiting for you, Doctor Goldszmit."

The Doctor greeted her, said that he was feeling well and introduced us. She looked at us and didn't know what to say. Finally she blurted out, "Cute children." The Photographer winked at me, because *cute* was the last thing one could say about us.

The examination was short and uneventful. I lay on a table, they covered me with a large apron made of lead, and then they photographed my legs with a machine which didn't look anything like a camera. We didn't see the rays at all. The Photographer watched the technician; his face was serious and excited, while he constantly wiped his hands on the sides of his trousers.

After the X-ray we all looked at the pictures taken. We could see the bones which seemed like white pipes against a black background, and one of them had a sort of crooked grey circle. The Professor touched the scar on my leg where the wound used to be and explained that the wound had gotten infected and that the infection had spread to the bone. This was the reason for the pain in my leg and my limp.

The Doctor explained. "There is an infection there, due to bacteria."

It sounded as if it was curable.

"So this circle can be removed from the bone?"

"I'm sorry," said the Professor. "That is impossible."

"Not even by an operation?"

"No."

"So can the infection be cured in any other way?"

"We don't know how," said the Doctor sadly. "One day medication will be discovered which will be able to kill germs, and the inventor of this medication will not only save people from a lot of pain but also save lives. It will be a great step forward for humanity."

His words were full of hope but they didn't cheer me up at all. Antibiotics had not yet been invented, the infection could not be treated and I remained with my limp just the way I had come in.

The Doctor had prepared me for this, but still I was very disappointed.

The Photographer was also disappointed. He repeated what the technician had told him, about the rays penetrating the bones and about the shadow they create, which is the white part of the X-ray, and said that he had expected to see something different.

"What exactly did you expect to see? Dwarves, sorcerers?" mocked the Professor. Perhaps his feelings were hurt because his photographs were not appreciated. The Doctor explained to the Professor that our Photographer was interested in technology but that first and foremost he was an artist. The Photographer nodded. He seemed to be pleased with the explanation.

On our way out, when we walked along those endless corridors, the Doctor explained that the hospital was part of the Warsaw University Medical School. "This is not a school for magicians and miracles," he said sadly, laying his hand on my shoulder. "What a pity!"

What a pity, indeed! I thought to myself even though I didn't believe in miracles.

The Doctor accompanied us to the station and then returned to the hospital to meet some medical students on their pediatric internship. The Photographer and I went back on the tram. In case the malicious rumors about my mother had reached his ears, I told him the real story of my limp.

"I too was a thief," he said, "before I arrived at the orphanage and became..." He searched for the right words to describe what had happened to him. Finally he said that at the orphanage he became a good person. Smiling he reverted to Yiddish, and said, "*Von a wilde Chaje zu a Mentch*" [*From a wild animal to a good human being.*]

I sensed he was trying to find something to say to cheer us up, when he ventured a hopeful prediction, one day X-ray machines would be able to cure ailments, not just reveal them. "Pictures don't come out beautiful on this X-ray, so at least they should be of some use."

I thought it was a pity that the Photographer was not my guardian instead of Josek.

"Do you want to get off at the camera shop?" he asked. "Perhaps the shopkeeper will allow you to hold the Retina."

I wasn't feeling well. My head was throbbing with pain. It was so cold that I felt like the roots of my hair had frozen onto my scalp under my cap. And cameras were of no interest to me at that moment. Still, I agreed. This was a big mistake. Something terrible happened to me in the camera shop. Suddenly, without any warning, I lost my mind.

13

What was I thinking? That I could run? That the infection in my bone had suddenly been cured? That the Photographer would appreciate my courage? That he would admire me? Why should he? Because he too had once been a thief? And the Doctor? Didn't I know he would be disappointed with me? Had I forgotten that he had warned me that the children's court could expel me for stealing? And how would Josek react? And Rosie? And Itcho? And Miss Steffa? And what if they told Mira to come and fetch me?

The truth is that at that moment, I didn't think of any of these things. I only noticed that the shopkeeper was repulsive, and maybe I realized that a million years would go by before the Photographer could save 300 Zloty. Seems to me my brain simply stopped working when I did the stupidest thing I could have done. I tried to steal the Retina.

At first, we stood by the shop window and the Photographer pointed to various cameras, the Retina first of course. He talked about lenses and shutters and all sorts of other technical stuff. The shopkeeper, a stout elderly man with greasy hair, joined us outside, looked at us, clapped his hands and made all kinds of whistling sounds, as if we were a couple of alley cats that had entered his kitchen, and not people who were standing on a public pavement, looking, one of us with real admiration, at the cameras in his shop-window.

The Photographer greeted him politely. "You again?" was the answer he received. The Photographer was not offended; at least he didn't behave as though his feelings had been hurt. He told the shopkeeper that we had just returned from the hospital where I had had my leg X-rayed. The shopkeeper looked at him crookedly. The Photographer said he had told his friend, meaning me, about the Retina. The shopkeeper snorted in contempt. I wanted to spit in his face and run off, but then the shopkeeper made a small gesture with his fat hand and the Photographer smiled and entered the shop. I followed.

The shop was empty, brightly lit and heated, and the shopkeeper stood next to us and listened to the long-winded explanations the Photographer gave me about his favorite camera. He probably realized that the Photographer was not just a poor boy - anyone could see that - but a true enthusiast who knew no less about cameras than him. He stretched out his arm towards the Retina in the shop window and gave it to the Photographer.

"If you drop it, it will be the end of you!" he warned.

I shifted my weight from the painful leg to the other one. Suddenly it was difficult to stand.

The Photographer held the camera as though it was a diamond; Not that I knew how you hold a diamond, I had never held a precious stone in my life! He said that one day in the summer, he would climb a tall tree with the Retina, lie across a branch and photograph the children in the schoolyard.

"The picture will look as though a bird took it," I said. My teeth began chattering from the cold.

"Exactly!" the Photographer was glad I understood what he meant. "A bird's eye view," he enthused.

"Do you think there's any chance you'll have 300 Zloty by summer?" chuckled the shopkeeper.

The question clipped our wings, so to say. Where indeed would the Photographer find 300 Zloty? It was clear that he would never be able to save this sum.

The Photographer passed the beloved Retina to me and at that very moment a man and woman entered the shop. He wore a three-piece suit and a broad-brimmed felt hat, and she was enveloped from head to toe in a thick grey fur coat. All of a sudden, the shopkeeper's demeanor changed completely. He became friendly or rather fawning. His voice as sweet as honey, he asked the *distinguished* people how he could be of service, whether they had ever been in his shop before, if they wanted to buy a camera to commemorate a special event, or if they wanted him to take photographs for them.

And then it just happened: I pushed the woman against the shopkeeper, she tripped, moaning in pain, and I burst out of the shop as though I had been shot from cannon, holding the Retina in my hands. "Run, run," I shouted to the Photographer who had stepped out of the store behind me. I moved quickly, not as fast as I used to, but fast enough, in spite of the pain and the limp.

"Stop!" shouted the Photographer.

"Run to the tram," I shouted back. Turning my head for a second I saw the Photographer running towards me with the shopkeeper close on his heels. The two customers had left the shop and went in the other direction. The shopkeeper could not run more than a few yards. He stopped and cursed, breathing hard, "You stinking thieves! You'll go to jail! Help! Stop them! Stinking thieves."

In a few moments, the Photographer caught up with me. I handed him the camera, but instead of running towards the tram station he grabbed the Retina and pushed me back with great force.

I fell onto the frozen pavestones. My head was spinning, and the pain in my leg got worse, as if it was on fire. Through the black spots dancing in front of my eyes I saw the Photographer as he ran towards the wheezing shopkeeper and pushed the camera into his hands. Instead of thanking him, the shopkeeper tried to beat him. The Photographer freed himself and ran towards me. He picked me up by my collar and pulled me quickly towards the tram. I could hardly move my legs.

The Photographer's face was hard and gray. He bit his lips with his huge teeth. Neither of us spoke a word.

The Photographer dragged me by my collar from the tram to the orphanage. Only when we were in the hall did he let go of me. Hella, the curly-haired tutor, was sitting at the table.

"You're late," she announced, without lifting her head from the papers in front of her. "Complaints can only be filed from 3 to 6 o'clock. It is now 6.15."

"He tried to steal a camera which costs 300 Zloty," the Photographer blurted out. "He turned me into an accomplice against my will."

Now Hella lifted her head slowly, her curls covering her face. The two of us looked as though we had just returned from battle, and this was indeed a most serious complaint. Hella took a clean sheet of paper and wrote down the Photographer's name and his complaint. Then she wrote down my name and asked me to tell her my version of the story. I remained silent. "Is this what happened?" she asked.

I nodded.

"Do you want to say anything in your defense?"

"No."

"I have to pin this on the notice board," she explained, twisting her curls into a bun. "The judges have to understand your side of the story. Tell me, did you want this camera very much?"

"No."

"Was there a misunderstanding?"

"No."

"Perhaps you thought that the Photographer expected you to do this?"

"No."

"So what, then?"

"I'm sorry," was all I could say.

The Photographer didn't even look at me when he left the room.

14

When Josek finished scolding me he turned to shout at the Photographer, and then at Hella. Why didn't she come to him before posting the complaint on the notice board? Didn't she know that I was new here? That I was under his supervision? Couldn't she see that I needed him? He shouted and stamped his feet and no longer sounded self assured or self satisfied. And all because of me.

Hella said she would file a complaint against him if he didn't stop shouting. Her feelings were really hurt.

"Please, calm down," said Rosie to Josek, glancing icily at me with her bright blue eyes. Josek took some deep breaths, tried to smile at me but his mouth would not cooperate. He suggested we go into the quiet room to talk things over. Rosie joined us, and so did Itcho and Hannah. We sat at one of the homework tables.

Josek said, "I am your guardian, your instructor, your mentor, I am responsible for your actions." I got it: he was mortified by what I had done because it would reflect badly on him and ruin his image as the perfect guardian.

Josek continued. "I am partly to blame. I wanted to stay with Rosie and that is why I agreed to the Photographer's request to accompany you to the X-ray. But what was on your mind when you ran away with the camera?"

"What does it matter now?" asked Rosie. "The deed is done."

I thought she was right, and anyway I had no answers to his question.

"If we could understand what had happened," Josek said, "we could write something in your defense and post it on the notice-board, something which would help you in court."

"Hella wrote that he apologized to the Photographer," said Itcho. Even though he tried not to catch my eye, I felt that Itcho was on my side.

Josek sighed. "That's not enough. I'm not sure the judges will believe that he is truly sorry, because he is new here and they don't really know him. And also-"

"He is known as a thief," Rosie finished his sentence.

I felt like a hammer had come down on my head.

"In short, if there was something we could add, the judges would probably take it into consideration," Josek summarized the matter.

"Take into consideration? What exactly?" Rosie was even more severe.

I felt rather strange, as if a lump of dough were rising in my head and filling each nook and cranny. I couldn't get my thoughts and feelings straight. Everything in my brain was jumbled. Still, I wanted to explain. I moved my tongue in my dry mouth and blurted out a series of incoherent sentences: "The shopkeeper was disgusting. And then the broad-brimmed hat came in with the fur. In summer the Photographer will take pictures from the top of the tree. The Retina costs 300 Zloty. It isn't fair. If the X-ray is ugly, at least it should be able to cure. This is a medical school, not a miracle school. The infection cannot be treated. I came with a limp, I left with a limp. One day, they will discover medication for it. Born to run? Let's see you run. It isn't fair!"

And then, very quietly, I whispered, "A thief, the son of a thief." Finally, I fell silent and looked at Itcho. He lowered his eyes, embarrassed by the string of disjointed sentences I had uttered.

"For some reason, I thought you could articulate yourself better than that," Rosie remarked cynically.

She was right. I was the quiet kind, but when I had something to say I was always very clear. Now, for some reason I wasn't.

Hannah, who had been sitting with her shoulders hunched forward, straightened up and said, "I think I understand. He went for an examination. The results were disappointing. This wasn't a miracle school, but a medical school, and he left just as he came in, with a limp, and no hope for a cure."

She took a deep breath and continued. The words poured out of her like warm water. "Then, in the camera shop, the shopkeeper was disgusting and the camera the Photographer wanted cost 300 Zloty. So, because of the disappointing examination, the disgusting shopkeeper, and the expensive camera, Janek felt that it was all unfair, so he tried to compensate himself or the Photographer or both of them. That is why he tried to steal the camera."

They all looked at her as if she had deciphered a secret code. Me too. Until she explained it all, I hadn't connected the disappointing examination results to the theft. But she was right.

Hannah looked into my eyes and asked, "Did I understand correctly, Janek?"

I nodded.

"Thank you, Hannah'le," said Josek.

"Yes," said Itcho.

"You forgot to say he was a thief, the son of a thief!" said Rosie, hammering away at me once again.

"Did you have to say that?" Josek hissed and stamped his foot.

"Janek said it himself, at the end of his grand speech," she said, mocking me, and then added scornfully, "Let's stop pretending. It's not as if we didn't know he is a thief, his whole neighborhood knows he's a thief."

Another hammer and another.

"A thief, the son of a thief," Rosie repeated.

"Don't involve parents in this," mumbled Itcho, trying to be funny.

Rosie got angry again. "There is no place among us for people like Janek, and there is no reason that Josek should be responsible for him."

"Rosie, I just want to write something in his defense," Josek tried to mollify her. "He wasn't able to explain himself to Hella, and I want him to have a fair trial."

"I hope the judges judge him harshly," she almost screamed. "This is not an orphanage for juvenile delinquents, and that is what he is."

"And all your lofty words about helping the weak, where is all of that now?" retorted Josek.

"Help? Of course we should help," she replied sharply. "But not when the weak hurt the rest of the community."

"He deserves another chance just like anyone else here," answered Josek.

"He hurts the weak and the strong," she interrupted. "And, in case you haven't noticed, he is hurting you!"

They called me *the weak* but I didn't care. The lump of dough which was my brain clearly realized one thing – I had been wrong about Josek. Until that moment, I had been sure that whatever Josek did, he did because he wanted to earn extra points and to prove how virtuous he was. I had had no doubt that he made an effort with me only so that everyone would realize what a wonderful guardian *he* was. That wasn't true! That wasn't the reason. He really wanted me to get another chance. I had been wrong about Rosie too. Suddenly I was so ashamed, not only because of what I had done but also because of what I had been thinking.

In a calmer tone Rosie asked Josek, "Why should we write anything on his behalf? He should write it himself if he has anything to say in his defense." Josek did not reply. He just looked at her. There was silence in the room. As we watched them quarrel I felt that Hannah, Itcho and I were their audience.. I didn't want to remember that I had wanted to steal her away from him.

"Am I not right, Hannah'le?" asked Rosie.

"I think that this time you are wrong," replied Hannah softly.

"It is just that he can hardly explain himself verbally, so how will he be able to do it in writing?" said Itcho hesitantly. It was clear that he was slightly afraid of Rosie, but I was right in feeling that he was on my side.

"So why don't you write it for him?" she smiled wickedly. Her suggestion was full of evil, for it was quite clear that Itcho with all his spelling mistakes would not have the courage to post anything he had written on the noticeboard. He liked to make people laugh, but he did not want to turn himself into a joke.

"What's wrong with you?" murmured Josek.

"Just imagine what would have happened if the camera had been broken," Rosie's voice grated on our ears. "Who would have paid the 300 Zloty?!" She didn't look beautiful anymore.

Again, there was silence.

"Right!" declared Rosie. "The Doctor! The money would have come from our funds."

"But it didn't happen," Josek raised his voice. "The camera was not damaged."

"I shall write a few words in his defense," Hannah suddenly spoke up.

"It's alright," I finally succeeded in moving my tongue in my mouth. "I'll... I'll write. I will explain that..."

"Perhaps he got sick," I heard Itcho saying, but his voice seemed far away, as if the dough in my head was now filling my ears from the inside.

"He stole because he was sick, you mean sick in the head?" chuckled Rosie. "What a wonderful excuse! Insanity is so convenient!"

I was blinded by the light in the room.

"You are evil," I heard Josek saying.

"No, I'm not!" Rosie's voice rang through the dough in my ears.

"He is really sick," I heard Hannah as if through a bottle, or a deep well. "Look at him!"

They looked at me. Their eyes grew wide open with surprise, as if I had suddenly turned into a pig.

And just then, I passed out.

15

Rosie was right about one thing: It is sometimes very convenient to be sick. True, you feel lousy and there are aches and pain, but you don't have to make any effort, you don't have to do anything.

I didn't choose to be sick, but my illness – I had contracted the mumps – gave me respite from everything, even from myself. My neck and throat hurt and I suffered from chills because of the high fever. I felt as though my head was full of dough, my eyes burned and the grey circle in my leg hurt like hell. I know it sounds crazy, but in spite of all these unpleasant sensations I managed to get some rest.

Every now and then the Doctor put a wet cloth on my forehead or dribbled a few drops of water into my mouth. I wasn't worried whether he was angry with me or whether I would be expelled, I wasn't even afraid to die. And that was strange, because in the past when Mira or I were sick, I was always afraid we would die.

Now I was completely calm, and this calm was only disturbed by the dreams I had occasionally. They were vivid and disturbing, because they were a mixture of different things with no connection to one another: Someone at the orphanage threatened Beautiful Rosie with a knife, the Photographer lay across a branch, high atop a tree that had grown in the middle of the great hall, and took photographs, and then Staszek tried to jump on a moving tram and a strong arm pushed him onto the street, and Shmulik cried all the time, and Mira leaned her cheek against Josek's square head, and a jagged-toothed smile appeared around the crooked circle in my leg. None of it made any sense.

I was in this state for a whole night, drifting between a deep, pleasant slumber and nightmares. When I opened my eyes to a new morning I didn't know where I was.

I wasn't in the dormitory of the orphanage nor in that of the shelter. Neither was I on the mattress in my grandmother's house. I was lying on a sofa in a small room with a high ceiling, a huge bookcase, a narrow bed which had been made up, a heavy wooden desk and a huge window. Someone was standing with his back to me looking out of the window at the grey morning outside. I sat up in bed with difficulty and then he, the Doctor, turned round towards me. I was in his room, in the attic. He came closer and laid a dry warm hand on my forehead and said, "At last the temperature is coming down."

My throat and ears hurt and I felt intense pain in my leg. I don't know why, but all of a sudden I thought that it had been amputated during the night. I didn't have the strength to pull back the blanket and look. I lay back and asked, "Did they take off my leg?"

He looked startled. "No! No! Why do you ask that?!"

My mouth was dry. "I once read in the paper about people with no arms or legs who felt intense pain in the amputated limbs."

"That's true," said the Doctor put his hand behind my neck and helped me sit up and drink some water from the glass he offered me. "It's called *phantom pain*. But you are suffering from the infection in the bone. The pain is terrible, I know."

I nodded. I took some more sips of water which hurt my throat as I swallowed.

"I gather you ran with no pity for your leg," the Doctor said sadly. "And now the infection has flared up again."

"Is that why I am here?" I asked and signaled with my head that I didn't want any more water.

"No, you're here because you caught the mumps and you had a very high temperature and I wanted to keep an eye on you."

"What is mumps?"

"It's a contagious disease. The lymph nodes under the ears and in the throat are swollen. Do you want to have a look in the mirror?" He handed me a small mirror. Everything was swollen: my neck and the lower part of my face. I did look like a pig.

"Am I going to die?"

"No," he answered confidently. "The disease is now at its peak, but in a few days it will pass."

"Doctor, I am so sorry, really sorry."

"I know," he said while examining my swollen lymph nodes. His touch was very gentle, but it still hurt. My eyes filled with tears. "I am not crying," I declared. Now I think it's silly but then I didn't want anyone to see me cry.

"That is your temperature rising again," he said, explaining the tears.

I wanted to ask him about my upcoming trial, but I was too weak.

"May I stay here a little while longer?" I managed to ask. I was feeling so sick.

"Yes," he said, tucking the blanket around my shoulders. "Later, when you're better, we'll transfer you to the sick bay."

I dropped off to sleep. When I woke, it was dark. My throat, eyes, neck, ears and the circle in my leg were all on fire. I looked at the Doctor. He was sitting at his desk writing, a small lamp lighting up the room. Even though he was concentrating on his work, he sensed that I had woken up and turned his head towards me. "How do you feel, Janek?"

Without me having to say so he knew I was feeling lousy. He helped me limp to the bathroom and drink a few sips of water. Then he laid a fresh cold compress on my forehead and said everything would be alright.

Through chapped lips I said, "The judges will charge me under clause 900, or even 1,000." Josek had explained the penal code of the children's court to me dozens of times, and I knew that clauses 900 and 1,000 were the most severe. These were the clauses that led to expulsion, except if someone agreed to be the guardian of the delinquent under caution. I was sure that Rosie had already convinced Josek that I had caused him only difficulties, and that he would not volunteer to take me on again after the verdict.

"Why do you think so?" the Doctor asked.

"You yourself said that stealing is a severe offence and could be grounds for expulsion. Besides, judges can be very cruel." I thought of my father's judge. Why did he send him to prison for so many years? He had only stolen, he hadn't hurt anyone, or perhaps he had? I knew nothing of my father's crimes. I just remembered that Mira said that if we had had any money, we could have hired a good lawyer for him.

The Doctor said that the judges at the orphanage were neither cruel nor soft-hearted, but impartial, and the sincere repentance I had shown would probably be taken into consideration. "Our law is based on the principle that it is always best to forgive," he added.

"But I have the reputation of being a thief!" I explained.

He didn't say: "No, you don't," or: "You yourself are to blame for that," or: "In our court we are not biased. You will be judged as if you do not have that reputation." He did not refer to my past at all. He just said, "I have a suggestion." And then he told me that he sometimes made a deal with children who misbehaved in a manner which caused unpleasantness to themselves and to others, behaviors which they could not control.

For example, a boy who curses constantly because that is what he is used to. Other children keep their distance, their feelings are hurt, they are angry. The boy himself would like to stop cursing but fails. Then the Doctor asks him if he would be prepared to give up cursing some of the time. Let's say the boy curses ten times a day, and now he is willing to wager that he can keep the cursing down to only four or five times a day. If the boy can hold out for a week he wins the wager and even gets a prize, a little money or some sweets, if he is very young. The wagering continues, decreasing the number of curses, until the boy stops cursing altogether.

"It works," claimed the Doctor. "Some children come here with negative behavior such as cursing, spitting, hitting. It is as though they are addicted to these bad behavior patterns. They would actually like to stop them immediately, but sometimes it is easier to go slowly. I suggest you wager with me on thefts. We shall decide what you may steal – let's say, apples – and how many times per week. What do you say?"

I thought it over for a little while. "Your suggestion might work for some children, but not for me," I finally replied. "I don't steal against my will. Up to now I only stole things I needed, newspapers and food and things with which I paid protection money at the Shelter. Sometimes I enjoyed stealing, I admit, but only because of my fast getaway. Only because I could disappear in a flash. That was my big advantage."

He listened attentively, concentrating on my words.

"There is a boy in our neighborhood," I told him, "who is an excellent thief. His great advantage is his size, he is tiny. He is ten years old but small and thin as if he were only five. He can enter through a narrow window, through the chimney. They say he can wriggle through the space between the door and the floor, that's an exaggeration, of course. This boy can enter houses through tiny openings. I hear that he has started working with a gang. They pay him to open the doors for them from the inside. Anyway, should this dwarf suddenly grow, he would lose his relative advantage."

"And you lost your relative advantage.... Your ability to run fast," he said. "So your problem is solved."

"I wish it was so," I whispered.

My long speech had exhausted me completely. If not for my high fever I would have told him that stealing was in my blood; perhaps I had inherited this trait from my father. Mira sews like our mother and I steal like our father.

He gave me a harsh look and said, "Stealing is not something you inherit."

"Isn't it?" I asked.

"I am a physician, so I understand such matters. There are quite a few things, physical and behavioral, that pass from one generation to the next. But not stealing. It is not in your blood. You will only be a thief if you decide that you are one. You have the freedom of choice."

I liked that expression, *freedom of choice*. My eyelids were so heavy they closed on their own.

"You are a free person," he said. "Free as a bird."

I fell asleep again, but this time I didn't sleep deeply. On the contrary - my sleep was light and thin like a potato peel, without any dreams at all. Just all kinds of thoughts running through my head, about thefts and races, and what does and does not pass from parent to child, and the freedom to choose.

I awoke to a new day, this time without any fever at all. I saw the Doctor standing at the window with his back to me. He was feeding the birds and giving them some water in a bowl. He watched them fly towards the window sill and land to have an early breakfast.

"They are mainly sparrows," he said without turning round. "They know what time I prepare their meal, and they know that there is plenty for everyone. In spite of that they sometimes fight over the crumbs and the stronger birds attack the weaker ones. That makes me angry. Sometimes I have to interfere."

"That was my last theft," I announced loudly, and then I did something I had never done before or since. I swore an oath on my mother's name.

He closed the window and smiled a small smile.

"Did you know that most people – when they are very sick, when they are delirious with fever or pain – call upon their mother?"

That surprised me so much that I hardly noticed that he had not reacted to my announcement not to steal ever again.

"Even someone who never knew his mother?" I asked. Of course I was thinking of myself.

"Yes. And even if the mothers were hard or cruel. And not only children..." He looked into the distance and continued, "I was a soldiers' doctor during the war between Russia and Japan and also during the World War. All of the wounded I treated, young soldiers and older officers, called out to their mothers when they suffered intense pain or had a high fever."

"What, adults also call out to their mother?"

"Even old people," he answered and smiled with his kind eyes. "When they are really sick they want their mother."

"Did I also call out for her?" I asked, hoping I did.

He turned towards the window, opened it for a moment and scattered some more crumbs.

"No," he said. "You called out for Mira."

16

Hannah was brought up by her grandparents until she was seven years old. They loved her and cared for her, but as time went by, things became more and more difficult for them. They were growing old and Hannah, without meaning any harm, always reminded them of their great tragedy. Hannah discovered what had happened to her parents only when she was five years old. One of her cousins told her that her mother fell in love with a non-Jewish boy. Someone had told her grandparents that her mother and her boyfriend were seen walking together in the park. They were very angry and forbade her to continue seeing him. His parents were also not delighted, to say the least, with their son's Jewish girlfriend. The young couple, and indeed they were very young, only 17 years old, decided to run away together. But the boy disappeared before they had a chance to carry out their plan. Hannah's mother was pregnant and stayed with her parents till Hannah was born, and then she too ran away, leaving the baby behind. The grandparents acted as if their daughter had died. They never talked about her. They never mentioned Hannah's father either, but once she heard her aunts talking among themselves, saying that Hannah looked exactly like a Polish farm girl, the spitting image of her father. That made Hannah very sad. She thought that if she had resembled her mother rather than her father, her grandparents would have found it easier to look at her.

Hannah had no idea whether her parents were living together or not, whether they were in Warsaw or somewhere else in Poland. Or perhaps they lived in some other country. Once, someone told her that he had heard from someone who had heard from someone else that her mother had gone to Buenos Aires in Argentina. This way or that, Hannah was sure that her mother was dead, for otherwise she would have surely sent her a letter, or some sign or gift. Perhaps she would have followed her while walking back from school, or peeped through the school's fence. But Hannah never received a letter or a sign, and she was sure she had never been followed. As for her father, Hannah decided to believe that he had not run away because of the pregnancy. If that was the case she would have been offended for herself, her mother and for him. She refused to think of him as such a bad person.

"I don't know why I am telling you all this," she said embarrassed.

"It's because you are ill," I said. "Because of the mumps." I too had told the Doctor all kind of things I wouldn't have dared to tell if I had been well, but I didn't regret it.

"True," agreed Hannah. "But that's only because I can't read now. My eyes are burning."

On the table was a pile of daily newspapers for me and three books for Hannah. We sat on the landing between the first two floors, overlooking the great hall. This was the ideal place to pass the time when we were sick. There was no danger of the other children catching whatever we had, but we were not completely isolated. We could take part in what was going on in the big hall and we could see and hear everybody, even talk to them. But mainly we talked to each other.

"Don't think that Rosie is a bitch," said Hannah.

"In the beginning I thought that Rosie was someone special," I admitted. "She was nice to me, sharing all those grand ideas of hers, but now I know that she is just a hypocrite."

"She is not. She is just scared."

"Scared?" I laughed. "Of me?"

75

"She is always afraid that things might not work out for her."

"How is that connected to me and to what I did?"

Hannah sighed. "It's difficult to explain."

Next to us on the mezzanine, little Nathan, another mumps victim, was napping. He was seven years old with a shaven head and side-locks like those of Orthodox Jews, which he tucked behind his ears. Hannah told me that Nathan had come to the home only two months earlier (she, too, called the orphanage *home*). The little boy had a high fever and was mumbling to himself in a mixture of Polish and Yiddish, giggling softly every now and then. We looked at him and smiled at each other with our swollen faces.

"Hannah'le, Sweetie, how are you?" Rosie's sharp voice resounded from below.

It was noon and the children were all returning from school.

Hannah ran to the banister to tell Rosie that she was better, that the Doctor had said that she only had a light case of mumps. Her temperature was not too high and she was just waiting for the ugly swelling to go down.

And then I heard Josek calling me. I approached the banister and looked down.

"How are you my friend?" he asked.

"Better," I replied.

Rosie and he stood about a meter apart, looking up at Hannah and me. They didn't exchange a word or a glance. Hannah told me that they had broken up after their noisy quarrel in the quiet room.

"Don't worry, Janek, everything will be fine," Josek promised.

I tried not to nag and ask how my case was coming along, but I could not restrain myself. I didn't want Rosie to hear what I had to say because she was probably still angry with him and hated me, but my future depended on two things – the trial and the vote on my status. I couldn't go back to Mira and Staszek, and I feared that I would not be able to survive on the street. I had seen children who lived on the street or in hovels between buildings. They lived in hell. That is why I asked in a few words, as if in code, "The trial, the vote?"

Josek said, "The vote went well. I have just posted the results on the board. You had 35 minuses and 25 pluses. The rest were indifferent. That's okay."

"Really?" I asked, for I didn't quite understand. Hannah, who was still leaning on the banister, turned to me and said that as a start that was fine. Most of the children didn't know me yet, and that is why they were indifferent. "That's normal. The next vote will be in a year, and by that time people will have changed their minds about you," she explained

"But what about the trial?" I mumbled.

"All things considered, you came out well. Believe me, I was afraid for you." That was Itcho. He called out from the direction of the notice board as he rushed towards Josek and Rosie. He stood between them and puffed out his cheeks as if he, too, had the mumps.

"Do you feel the way you look?" he asked.

I laughed. Hannah left the banister and disappeared on the landing and Rosie turned her back on us and went towards the dining tables. Now only Josek and Itcho stood beneath the banister.

"Josek, I am so sorry," I said but the sound of the lunch bell drowned my apology.

The children began to sit down at the tables. I knew that soon we, the sick children, would also be served lunch. I could hardly swallow anything except liquids. That is why we were served chicken soup with noodles which slipped down our throats easily. Nathan, the little boy with the side-locks, joined Hannah and me.

"This is so good," he said after noisily slurping the noodles into his mouth. "It reminds me ... of mother." His eyes filled with tears and his nose dripped.

"It's because of the fever." I tried to console him, just like the Doctor had comforted me when I was ashamed of crying.

"Or because of the hot soup," added Hannah.

Nathan wiped his nose and eyes on his sleeve. "I miss my mother".

Hannah stroked his head and whispered to me, "Sometimes I forget that we are orphans." And to Nathan she said, "Do you want me to read you a story after lunch?"

He smiled his toothless smile. A week earlier, he had lost three baby teeth.

Hannah said she wanted to be a librarian when she grew up. Even now she tried to get assigned to library duty as often as she could. But other children also liked library duty, so she had no choice other than to share her sessions with them. She told me that she began reading books at the age of four. She used to accompany her cousin, who was the cleaner at a public library. In the beginning, while her cousin cleaned the library, Hannah leafed through the books and looked at the pictures, but slowly she began to recognize the letters of the alphabet and make connections between the letters and the sounds they make, so that she finally began to read.

Sometimes the cousin worked all morning, until the library opened and the librarians came to work. Other times, the cousin left her there and went to clean the house across the street, and came back for her after a few hours. There was a nice librarian there who opened a library card for Hannah so that she could borrow books and also helped her choose books she thought Hannah would like. Hannah told me that this librarian taught her how important it was to choose the right book; if you give a child an unsuitable book, a book that might bore him, or might be too difficult for him, the child might lose interest in reading and won't want to try reading another book. But if you choose well and give the child a book which will fascinate him, you will open his heart to other books.

I said I preferred newspapers. I like the short paragraphs and the fact that everything that's printed is true, or supposedly. I like to read about things that are really happening or have happened before. Hannah said she preferred fiction, long novels which take a while to read and are not finished in ten minutes. She doesn't care whether the story is based on real events, but she has to be completely absorbed by it. With a newspaper, she added, there is nowhere to go, because you're invariably reading mostly about the place in which you live.

We could have gone on with our discussion about books and newspapers, but the Doctor arrived on the landing. He wanted to know how we were, whether we had eaten, if we had a fever, and if the swelling in our throat had gone down. Nathan gave him a hug, and Hannah asked him which book would be suitable for Nathan, as he knew him better. "Perhaps something by Kornel Makuszynski," suggested the Doctor. Hannah smiled. She was pleased with herself, because she too had thought about this writer, and the Doctor was a writer himself.

"Could you please check if *The Adventures of Matolek the Billy-Goat* has not been checked out from the library?" asked Hannah.

"Yes, agreed the Doctor, "you are quite right, Matolek is very appropriate."

She blushed, full of professional pride.

"I almost forgot," said the Doctor, turning to me and putting a batch of newspapers on the table. I wanted to ask you if you're familiar with *Little Review*."

"No, I only know the *Daily Review*".

"*Little Review* is a children's newspaper included in the weekend edition of the *Daily Review*."

I picked up the newspaper. "This doesn't look like a children's newspaper," I said.

"True!" The Doctor smiled, pleased. "That's exactly the point. This is a real newspaper written for children and teenagers, without fairy tales or drawings. The journalists at *Little Review* are also children. I would like to hear what you think about it. Have a look and tell me what you really think. Just ignore the fact that I founded it, okay?" He winked and went downstairs to find the book that Hannah had requested for little Nathan.

I began looking at the headlines in *Little Review*. In the background I heard Nathan say he wanted to be a baker when he grew up. This was the most common ambition among us poor children – to be in a place where there is always bread, so we would never be hungry. Nathan said that his mother used to tell him a story about a little boy who slept in a loaf of bread. He wanted Hannah to tell him that story, but she had never heard of it. Hannah said that perhaps his mother invented the story especially for him. Nathan liked that.

"Many children seem to know what they want to be when they grow up," I thought out loud. "Nathan wants to be a baker, Josek a youth counselor, Rosie a lawyer, you a librarian. I have no idea. Nothing really interests me."

"You must be joking," said Hannah with a wide grin. "What about all these newspapers? Even the Doctor wants to hear your opinion about his newspaper."

"What's your point?" I asked.

"Just as it's clear that I'm a book person, it is also clear that you are a newspaper person. It's something you are really interested in. It also seems that the Doctor thinks you understand something about it."

I felt as if I was puffing up with pride.

Mischa, who was on library duty, ran up the stairs and handed Hannah the book she had asked for. She began reading to Nathan with a deep hypnotizing voice. I listened for a while and then I became engrossed in the issues of *Little Review*. I felt good, really good, because of what the Doctor had said to me, and now Hannah, too. I'm telling you, this mumps business is the best thing that could have happened to me.

17

How I wished the Photographer would withdraw his complaint. I was told that there were a few days between filing a complaint and the actual trial during which the complaint could be retracted. Studying the notice board I learnt that often complaints never reached the court. Usually people calmed down or the plaintiff had a change of heart, accepted the apology of the defendant. But the Photographer, who had never lodged a complaint against anyone during his six years at the orphanage, said he felt a crime had been committed against him and demanded a trial. He didn't talk to me and I was ashamed to talk to him. It was clear he could never go back to the camera shop and look at his beloved Retina through the shop window. I wondered whether he found it in another shop window or whether he was still looking at it, from afar.

I was no longer afraid the court would expel me. Josek reassured me on that matter. He said that even if the court decided to proceed under clause 1,000, he would appeal. If the appeal was rejected he would take upon himself the responsibility for what I had done and demand I be granted a second chance. Strange, not so long ago, on the day of the theft, I was unhappy that he was my guardian, and now I thought how lucky I was to have him. On Friday night a boy passed around a hat with slips of paper with the names of the possible judges. Only children who were *fellows* or *residents*, were at least nine years old and, most importantly, had had no complaints lodged against them in the previous week, could serve as judges. I looked at the five slips of paper which had been pulled out of the hat. Later the names were posted on the notice board: Lezer, Itzik, Yulek, Sarah'le and Rosie.

I was appalled. Rosie could convince anyone of anything, just like a lawyer, and she was against me, perhaps now even more than before, as Josek had broken up with her because of me. The others I didn't know, only their faces. Sarah'le sat at the same table as I, but I hadn't had a chance to talk to her yet. I had no idea what they thought of me and of what had happened.

During the days leading to the trial, my heart and head felt frozen. On Saturday morning, when the trial finally began, it was as if blood rushed out of my face. My head felt like a large balloon swinging on top of my neck that was less swollen now. I had almost overcome the mumps. All the other complaints were dealt with before my case came up. They all seemed banal and unimportant: pushing, cursing, the most severe was dodging a turn of duty. Not a single complaint was as serious as mine. The highest clause was 200.

And then my turn came. We sat in that quiet room, one hundred and seven children, several tutors and the Doctor. It seemed they were all on tenterhooks to hear my verdict. They had all read the Photographer's complaint and what Josek had written in my defense. They also knew that the *royal couple* had broken up because of me.

Miss Steffa read the complaint against me and my apology and then turned to the judges. The first was Lezer. He looked over my head and uttered, clause 500. I felt as if I had stopped breathing and time stood still, until Miss Steffa called Itzik. "Clause 400," he said. Yulek spoke only after a series of coughs. He also said "Clause 400," and resumed coughing. Only when the cough subsided did Miss Steffa turn to Sarah'le, who looked from me to the Photographer and back again, as though she couldn't make up her mind. Finally, she, too, said, "Clause 400."

And then Miss Steffa turned to Rosie. Rosie kept silent for a long time until Miss Steffa called her again by name, and then she glared at Josek and said, "Clause 300."

Miss Steffa announced that the consensus was clause 400, and I felt as if a huge gust of air was sweeping the hall, from one end to the other. I sighed in relief. The hall was silent while Miss Steffa read the Judges' decision. They took in consideration the fact that I was new, that I had apologized, and took note of the special circumstances – which Josek had posted on the notice board, the circumstances that led to the theft. I listened to every single word but remained frozen in my seat.

Then Itcho hugged me. "It's a pretty severe clause, but things could have been worse." Rosie came over and said, "I am glad we were not too strict with you." She glanced at Josek who stood next to me. He dropped his gaze to the floor. "Anyone can make a mistake," she added, "I got angry, I spoke harshly, but we can forget that, can't we?" I nodded, coolly. Josek kept silent.

The Doctor arrived and rescued us from the awkward situation.

"Janek, before you go to visit your sister, please come by my office," he said.

He thought I intended to visit Mira, but of course I had no intention of doing so. I got nervous at once, but not because of the visit. Suddenly, I feared that he did not agree with the verdict. After all, no punishment attached, just a clause number. Perhaps, I thought, the children's court hands down a verdict, and the punishment is meted out by the adults.

Limping I followed him to the office. I stood there as tall and erect as I could. I 'm sure the Doctor didn't realize that I thought he was about to give me a beating as punishment. Had he known what I was thinking, he surely would have been very offended, for he was against violence especially towards children.

To my surprise he just asked me to take off my shoes. I did as I was told and then he handed me a different pair. One of the shoes had a slightly thicker sole than the other, intended for my limping leg. He asked me to try them on, which I did. I walked a few steps and stopped in amazement. Thanks to the lift on the shoe, I didn't limp at all.

"We can't cure the infection, so that you can run again," said the Doctor. "But I think the lift will help. You'll walk more evenly, and with less pain."

I took a few more steps, all the while looking down at my feet. What a wonderful feeling, just to be able to walk like everyone else, not to sink into one leg or drag it after the other. It seemed strange. Most of my life I had walked like everyone else, I had only been limping for a short time, but now I felt as if a million years had passed since I walked like everybody else.

"Is it comfortable?" asked the Doctor.

I nodded, and thought to myself, I am no longer a runner, no longer a thief, no longer lame. I am a new person. I walked on the spot, happy.

"Thank you," I mumbled and looked at my new shoes. From above, I couldn't see the difference between the two shoes. "Thank you," I repeated. Truth be told, I wanted to embrace him as little Nathan had done, but I have never been the hugging kind. Still, I lifted one hand towards him and then the other. He took both my hands in his warm and dry hands and said, "Now go show Mira. She will surely be happy for you."

I had no desire to visit her, but I felt I owed it to him. As soon as I arrived in the neighborhood I felt depressed, I don't know why. The carpenters didn't repair, the peddlers did not peddle. No one stood outside the shops, talking. The streets were almost deserted. The festive atmosphere of a Saturday afternoon could be felt everywhere. Soft white snowflakes were just beginning to fall. If the snow had piled up on the pavements, children would have come out to play, throwing snow balls and building snowmen, and surely someone would have recognized me.

You're not lame anymore, I told myself. So what do you care if someone sees you? I couldn't explain why I didn't want to meet anyone I knew. One of our neighbors, her head covered with a kerchief, saw me going into the courtyard between the houses. She nodded towards me but did not say a word before climbing the stairs to her apartment.

I went up the stairs and stood before our door. I heard Staszek's voice. He was lecturing, again."What do you think? That this has nothing to do with us? That if it didn't happen in our neighborhood, in our home or to our child, it doesn't affect us? You're mistaken! It will come here too, to each and every house." His voice alone made me angry. I couldn't hear Mira's voice, but I could imagine her biting her nails and listening to him, every so often tweeting a small tweet with a question mark at the end. Just as it had been when I lived with them.

What a pity that Staszek doesn't work on Saturdays, or go to the synagogue, or drink vodka in some bar and make his endless speeches there. Had I thought there was any chance of him leaving the house on this snowy Saturday afternoon, I would have waited on some street corner until he left. Then I would have knocked on the door and walked in tall and straight, with no limp at all, and would have told Mira everything that had happened to me since I had gone to Korczak's orphanage. Or maybe I wouldn't. Perhaps I wouldn't have entered even if Staszek were somewhere else. I was even angrier at her than at him. She was my sister, not he. I didn't think she deserved to hear about all the good things that had happened to me at the orphanage, like the new shoes, so she couldn't say, "I told you that your life would be better there," and with it she would clear her conscience.

I stood at the door for a few more minutes. I could imagine the inside of the apartment, small and cramped, dilapidated and cold, with mattresses on the floor and the tub full of laundry, so different from the large house I now lived in. I couldn't bring myself to go in, and I was sure that on the following Saturdays I wouldn't even come up the stairs. I slipped down the banister and walked quickly to the nearest tram station. The further I got, the better I felt. And I had plenty of time on my hands. I decided to join Itcho. He didn't go visiting on Saturdays because he had no family living in Warsaw. Actually I had no idea if he had family anywhere in the world. He never talked about his life before he came to the orphanage as if he had come from nowhere. Itcho went to the movies almost every Saturday, sometimes he saw the same movie several times. That Saturday he wanted to see a movie with Charlie Chaplin who was one of his heroes. The other was Israel Schumacher, a Yiddish comedian. Itcho had mentioned that he had attended several of Schumacher's performances without paying. That had been so much fun. He had told me that he felt that Chaplin and Schumacher were his real teachers, in the best sense of the word, not like the teachers at school, whom he hated.

Then he corrected himself. "My real teachers are Korczak, Schumacher and Chaplin. They've taught me all I'll ever need to know."

That Saturday, while sitting in the dark watching the movie, I noticed Itcho imitating Chaplin's gestures and facial expressions. I stretched out in my seat and concentrated on the movie and on the funny face of the English actor with the sad eyes and the square black moustache.

I've noticed he had the same moustache as Adolf Hitler, but Chaplin made us laugh and Hitler – who was still far away – was already making us anxious.

18

When the movie was over, it was still snowing. But it wasn't very cold, so Itcho, who was delighted that I no longer limped, suggested we go to the river. I was so glad to go to the Vistula. I hadn't been there in a long time, ever since I couldn't run. Near the river the wind was stronger but I didn't care. We pulled our caps over our heads and turned up the collars of our coats. We bought hotdogs in rolls at a small stand. Itcho asked the vendor for extra mustard and pickled cabbage. He chewed his roll and looked at the river. Then he sighed and said, "This is probably what they mean when they talk about the *miracle on the Vistula.*"

I was surprised. Was it possible he didn't know where the expression came from? I didn't want to embarrass him by asking if he hadn't heard about such an important chapter in our history. So I just told him the story of how, in 1920, the Russians were again preparing to conquer us minutes after we had regained our independence; and how our President Jozef Pilsudski left everything and led our soldiers into battle against the Russian army; how Pilsudski raised the moral of the soldiers and defeated the Russians right here, on the banks of the Vistula, causing them to retreat with their tails between their legs. The Russian army was defeated, and we, the Poles, were saved. And since then the battle was known as the *Miracle on the Vistula.*

Itcho listened, riveted, and just said, "Uh."

I continued. "I admire the president. He is a true hero. He takes care of his soldiers and of animals. I once read that he cried when his horse died on the battlefield."

I couldn't quite understand the expression on Itcho's face, so I asked, "Well, that says something good about him, doesn't it?"

Itcho nodded.

"And besides, he is also good to the Jews. He is sick now, and they say that if he dies, our condition will not be so good."

"I knew nothing of all of this," said Itcho. "Not that he is sick, not about his horse, not about the Russian army, not about the Vistula and not about the miracle."

I didn't want him to feel bad, so I said, "Well, the *Miracle on the Vistula* happened before we were born."

"Still, you knew about it."

"Only because I'm addicted to newspapers," I explained. I didn't point out that this was one of the things taught at school. I didn't want him to feel even worse.

He was quiet. I didn't know what to say either. So I told him that Hannah and I had an argument about which was better, newspapers or books. But this made things even worse.

"What a stupid thing to argue about," he said. "The main thing is to find a good story, and it doesn't matter if it is in a newspaper, a book or a movie!" He pointed towards the tram. "Let's go home," he said, depressed. But when we reached the station we didn't stop, just continued walking. I felt excited about walking without a limp but was a little afraid the inflammation would start up again if I walked too much, or too fast. But I didn't talk about it. I wanted Itcho to feel better. I felt it was my fault that he was sad.

"Soon it will be Hanukah," he said after a long silence. "I love that holiday."

"Because of the potato latkes and the doughnuts?" I asked. Food always gave me a thrill.

"Yes," he replied in a soft voice. "And also because of the story of the victory over the Greeks and the miraculous jug of oil. You too?"

"I never thought about it," I admitted.

"You haven't?" he got all excited again. "Some of the stories about the Jewish festivals are exaggerated, of course. The story of Passover is the worst. Those ten plagues: blood, frogs, and worst of all, the taking of the first born. And the story about God tearing the sea apart."

I thought that considering he had difficulty reading, he knew quite a lot of the biblical stories. He loved stories.

On Friday nights the Doctor always told a bedtime story, one week in the boys' room and the next in the girls' room. Sometimes it was a story from the book he happened to be writing, or a story someone else had written, or a fairy tale. Everyone's attention was riveted, even if the story was for the little ones, like *Puss in Boots*. Itcho was more excited than anyone else. He almost jumped from his bed when the Doctor told a story.

"But the Hebrews were liberated and became a free people," I said. "That is the most important part of the story of Passover."

"And what about Moses? Does it make sense to you that a mother puts her child in an ark and lets him float down the river never to see him again?"

"Yes, that was the only way she could save him."

" 'Miracle on the Vistula'," he looked at me askance. "This was a Miracle on the Nile." He became serious again. "I have a problem," he said.

I was glad, not because he had a problem, but because he wanted to talk to *me* about it. "I'm listening."

Itcho told me that Hella, the tutor, had asked him and a few other children to plan the Hanukah party. He agreed, of course, and he also agreed to take a role in a play. But quickly, things became complicated for him. Itcho found out that the play was not supposed to be funny.

"Why? Why did I have to argue about that?" Itcho said to me, and slapped his hand against his forehead. Anyway, he had argued and someone had said that he, Itcho, didn't want to put on a serious play, because he could only make people laugh but could not act at all. That had made him furious. "Charlie Chaplin can bring people to tears, not only tears of laughter but also tears of sorrow. That is what a great comedian is all about! He can break your heart!" Having said that, Itcho took it upon himself to participate in the play in any dramatic role on offer, even a tragic one if need be. Hella took some sheets of paper from her bag, a play the Doctor had written a few years before. She said she loved that play and thought that it would be wonderful to put it on, and would like to hear what the children thought. She asked Hannah to read the play aloud.

"Hannah'le read the play," Itcho continued. "And it really is a beautiful play, and her voice made it even more beautiful, it came to life, just like a movie."

"What happens in the play?"

"Not much. It's a conversation between two candles, one a regular everyday candle, used in a carpentry shop, or a shoemaker's shop, to cook by or to iron by. The other is a Hanukah candle. In any case the regular candle feels like nothing next to the Hanukah candle, which is festive and beautiful and used only once a year, and has such an important role in history that it can be proud of the Hanukah miracle and of his fathers, the holiday heroes. But the Hanukah candle does not want for the everyday candle to feel inferior, because its father is the workday. It says, 'Once a year I tell the story of the past, but you, you are the one that helps bring forth the future because your light enables everyone to work.' And then together they march and give light to all people... Oh, I'm ruining it when I tell it like that, it is much better written. I'm telling you, when Hannah'le reached the end there were tears in my eyes."

"So what's the problem?" I asked.

"It turns out that I insisted on a serious role before thinking it through. I'm used to being funny, to improvising... I am not... In short, I'll have to learn my lines by heart... Do you understand my problem?"

I did. If he can't read how is he going to learn his part by heart?

"I would have said that I don't want the part," continued Itcho, "but it's a beautiful play. You might find it strange, but it is challenging to play a candle, to bring it to life. Still, I can tell them that it's not for me."

"So that's what you should do."

"I don't want to!" Itcho was furious for a moment and then calmed down. "They wanted Hannah'le to play the part of the Hanukah candle because she read the part so beautifully?"

Suddenly the penny dropped. He loves her, he loves Hannah'le.

"She says she can't go on stage, she doesn't mind reading aloud but she can't go on the stage and play the part in front of everybody. She is shy. She will get confused. So I said to her, 'Don't worry, I'll help you.' Do you realize how stupid I was? Instead of saying that they can't force us to perform, I got myself even deeper in."

"How long is it till Hanukah?" I asked.

"Three weeks."

I thought for a moment and then said, "I think you have two options, both of them good. The first one is, I will help you. I will read your part to you a million times till you-know it perfectly."

"And the second option?"

"This one will be good for Hannah, too," I said and explained my plan. "Hannah will read the whole play aloud. I heard her reading when we were both sick with the mumps. You are right. She reads beautifully."

"Doesn't she?" he said, delighted.

"And you will play both parts. You might need two half costumes, or something like that."

"No problem. Sarah'le is in charge of the costumes," he said.

"In any case," I continued with the plan, "Hannah will sit at the side of the stage because she doesn't feel comfortable with everyone seeing her, and read the text, and you will skip from one character to the other, like Charlie Chaplin in a silent film."

His face relaxed. "There is one small problem," he said after a moment, this time with a smile. "The play takes place in the home of a girl who is sewing a festive shirt for her brother by the light of the everyday candle. She falls asleep and then the Hanukah candle knocks on the door."

I smiled.

"Right," he began talking in the high voice of a girl. "I'll also play the part of the sleeping seamstress."

"In the end it might turn out funny," I warned.

"Sure, but also sad!"

"You mean moving," I corrected him. "Because in the end both candles combine their light into one great flame to gladden the hearts of the spectators."

"At the end of the play Hannah will join you," I pretended to give stage instructions with dramatic gesture. "And you'll walk together like one candle to the front of the stage to take your bows in front of an ecstatic audience."

"You're the *Miracle on the Vistula,*" he said and hugged me tightly. Itcho was the hugging kind, and he didn't let go of my shoulders until we got onto the tram. Standing together in the aisle, rocking from side to side, we rode the tram home like two happy drunks.

19

The play was a huge success thanks to seven people: firstly, the Doctor who wrote it, and secondly, Itcho whose performance was excellent. I don't know much about plays, and it's hard for me to say exactly what Itcho did that was so wonderful, but when he played the part of the workaday candle everyone felt that here was a simple candle with an inferiority complex whereas when he played the Hanukah candle you could feel that here was a wise and noble candle with a glorious past.

Thirdly, Hannah deserved credit for her deep, honeyed voice and the way she read the parts. The Doctor said she had a radio-phonic voice. And that perhaps they would one day host a radio program together about a subject they both loved -- books. For a moment I was a bit envious, and I can bet I wasn't the only one.

Sarah'le, too, deserved some credit for creating the complicated costume that Itcho wore, a kind of cloak divided in two, a simple half like a workman's overall, and–a bright and shiny half, befitting a Hanukah candle. The stage designer was Izchak, the painter. He painted the house of the seamstress in brown and grey tones, like the interiors of poor people's houses. The lighting also played an important role. The photographer lit up the stage with two giant spot lights. Whenever Itcho switched roles, meaning candles, the lights changed with him.

And I got credit as well, for the idea of how to mount the play. The staging, in theatrical terms, was all mine. My name even appeared on the list of thanks that was distributed together with the play's program. I was pleased with myself, not only because the idea was a success but because it was born out of friendship.

Josek and Rosie sat in the row in front of me. In the middle of the show, I saw them holding hands. In the weeks following their quarrel, they had trod around each other with gloomy faces. Each of them waited for the other to take the first step and apologize.

"Such stubbornness," complained Hannah. "Rosie refused to forgive Janek and now Josek refuses to forgive her. Actually, they suit each other very well, both so stubborn."

I wished Josek and Rosie would make up. I felt bad because Josek was sad. I didn't care that much about Rosie's feelings but I wanted them to reconcile because that was what Josek wanted. And besides, I was tired of feeling guilty.

After the show Itcho and Hannah took their bows, and we clapped and whistled. They held hands and bowed again and again. Hannah's face was flushed and Itcho's eyes shone. We were in the great hall, and in the audience there were many visitors. They were rich people, benefactors of the orphanage, dressed in fine suits and dresses. I was told that the orphanage owed its existence to them. The guests seemed to be thrilled by the play. They approached Itcho and Hannah to shake their hands.

Afterwards we lit the Hanukah candles, sang songs and ate potato latkes. Itcho told me that the guests had asked him what his name was and that he had answered, "Itcho Schumacher."

I laughed.

"Perhaps it's not my real name," he said, "but it is the name that should have been mine."

"Not Chaplin?" I asked with a smile.

He remained serious. "I'm not joking. I am his son. I probably have several brothers and sisters all over Poland and perhaps in other countries too. Wherever Schumacher performs, the girls go crazy for him, and that's how it happened."

"Is there any factual basis to this theory?" I asked.

He touched my hand and nodded towards Miss Steffa. I realized she was looking at us sternly. We immediately joined in the singing, so as not to spoil the holiday for the little ones.

When we sang those Hanukah songs, especially the ones in Yiddish, I thought that Itcho was my first best friend. Of course I had had friends in the past, but things were different then, when I could still run. I was always something of a lone wolf. Mostly, it was just my sister and me. But now, with Itcho, and with the rest of them, I suddenly realized that I hadn't thought of Mira since I had almost visited her several weeks earlier. I felt distant from her and from the boy I had been in the past. It was like being a completely different person now, as if the person I was in the past had died.

20

"Come on, you geek, you have to listen to this!" Itcho pulled me from
the quiet room into the great hall.

The other children, who had sat by me studying, had long left the
room, but I was so engrossed in my homework that I didn't notice the
hours passing. Luckily the program had not yet begun, there were
still a few minutes, but everyone was already crowding around the
radio, waiting to hear the Doctor's voice. Until that afternoon, I did
not know that he had his very own radio program.

Itcho said, "Last year he read some stories in installments. That
was wonderful!" As the program began, I saw Itcho frown in
disappointment. The Doctor, whose soft voice had acquired a
metallic sound on the radio, chose to start with a letter he had
received from a concerned boy. The boy wrote that his parents beat
him constantly and that he couldn't wait to grow up so that he could
beat them up, too; perhaps the Doctor had an idea how to make them
stop beating him?

"Orphans have no such problems," someone joked. "Depends to
which institution they get sent," answered another. Both boys were
hushed into silence, and the room was quiet again. The Doctor said
that he disagreed with corporal punishment, especially when grown-
ups beat children, but he thought it was a bad idea for children to

beat up their parents. The Doctor suggested that the next time they get angry and threaten to beat him, he should ask them to count to ten before they raise a hand to him. Hopefully, once they calmed down, they wouldn't resort to blows. Only then did I understand the logic of the fights schedule posted on the notice board. The Doctor was a wise man. If after a quarrel you have to sign up to schedule a physical fight in a few days time, chances are that by then you will have calmed down and changed your mind. And indeed, the list of cancelled fights on the notice board was almost as long as the list of scheduled fights. I wondered if the Doctor's advice to the boy who wrote the letter would work and his parents would beat him less often. Josek said that many parents listened to the Doctor's program; surely there were some who wanted to stop beating their children, or at least beat them less often.

After replying to the letter, the Doctor told a story, but not in the usual manner. It sounded as if he was responding to a letter from a boy who squandered all his money and got into debt. It seemed as if the Doctor was talking to the boy, but he was actually telling the listeners how the boy had gotten himself into such a big mess, and how he could get out of it. I thought that this was a wonderful way to tell a story, it was like listening to one side of the conversation, but still understanding everything. Itcho too was satisfied. The program lasted for another quarter of an hour and then the announcer said that the program *The Old Doctor* would now be broadcast every Thursday afternoon at four. He gave the address of the radio station and invited listeners to send questions. He also promised that some of the Doctor's responses would be published in the radio station's newspaper *Antenna*. I thought it was a lovely name for a radio newspaper.

Later, while we were eating supper, I asked Josek why the program was called *The Old Doctor* without ever mentioning, neither at the beginning nor at the end, who the Doctor actually was.

"It *is* strange," Sarah'le, who sat opposite me, said, as if she was thinking aloud. "He is famous all over Poland. Many teacher seminaries invite him to give lectures, and the courts ask his advice in trials concerning juveniles. And all the newspapers ask him to write articles about education or publish his stories. How come the radio is not proud to announce that *The Old Doctor* is actually the famous writer and pedagogue Janusz Korczak?"

Josek said, "The Doctor claims he likes the name of the program because here, at the orphanage, he is called *The Doctor*, and he himself feels quite old, but..." He took a big bite of his omelet, and then continued, "Rosie thinks that the people at the radio prefer the public not to know that *The Old Doctor* is Janusz Korczak, because everyone knows Korczak is Jewish."

Rosie's explanation didn't make sense to me, not just because now I tended to disagree with every word she said, and not because I remembered that Staszek always suspected everyone, Christians and even many Jews, of hating Jews.

"Do you think that makes sense?" I asked Josek. He shrugged his broad shoulders and looked over the heads of the seated children towards where Rosie was seated.

Sarah'le said, "I think it does. The hatred of Jews is getting worse and worse." She spoke just like Staszek, I thought to myself. But a few days later I had to admit that she and Rosie and even Staszek might be right.

It happened on Sunday when we were all walking to school together. The children in the Christian schools studied on Saturdays and had the day off on Sundays. For us Saturday was a free day and Sunday was a regular school day. Jewish pupils who went to school on Sunday were conspicuous because of their school uniforms. Sometimes there was no trouble, but on some occasions they were cursed, spat on and even beaten by Christian children who had nothing better to do on their free day. When I could still run, the whole business didn't bother me; the worst that could happen was that someone would curse me behind my back.

But now I was part of a group, and on a street corner in the middle of the way to school, about ten bullies were waiting for us. The orphanage children were used to being hassled. To protect themselves they quickly formed a cluster, with the smaller children and the girls in the center and the older boys on the outside. Like one block we walked together swiftly past the waiting ruffians. They began throwing snowballs at us with bits of ice in them. We were attacked on all sides. Josek shouted, "Don't react, don't stop." He protected Rosie with his large body. "Did you hear me, Itcho? We don't want any trouble."

"Stinking Jews!" someone shouted.

"*Beilises*, go away!" another one called out. I didn't understand what he meant by *Beilises*, I've never heard this word before.

"Poland for the Poles," screamed another. That really made me mad, for we too were Poles. Then there was more shouting and cursing, mostly foul things about our parents.

Itcho walked close to Hannah who was covering her face. I too pushed myself towards the girls who were walking fast within the circle of older boys. I wanted to be part of the human shield, but unlike Josek with his broad shoulders and burly Itcho, I felt like a thin shoelace, that could do nothing to stop the icy snowballs from hitting their target. Our opponents aimed high and deep into our circle, hitting us on our heads and on our faces.

I thought to myself that had I been able to run I wouldn't have been hit at all, but I hoped that even if I could have run away, I would have chosen to stay, in order to be part of the protective ring. The thought made me feel good. I smiled to myself, and just then a little girl gazed up at me with a strange look on her face. The remains of a huge snowball were running down her cheeks and her chin was trembling as if she was about to burst into tears. She held onto my sleeve, and I didn't know what to do, so I said, "Don't worry, it's not so bad, we'll arrive at school in a moment."

21

In May of that year the president, Jozef Pilsudski, died. The Doctor read us the obituary he had written for the orphanage weekly. He wrote about the first days of Poland's independence, how Pilsudski succeeded in uniting many different factions and creating a new independent state without destroying people or their rights. He thought, just as I did, that Pilsudski was good for the Poles and for Poland. I had no idea whether he also feared that now, after Pilsudski's death, the situation of the Polish Jews would deteriorate. Those who did think so proved to be right. New laws curtailed the opportunities open to Jews to make a living and they became even poorer than before. Racism spread all over, and more and more people contracted it as if it were a contagious disease. Anti-Semitic sentiment was everywhere – in graffiti on city walls, in newspaper articles, in the look in people's eyes, in what was said and in what was done.

We too, felt that our situation had worsened because we suffered more harassment on Sundays. Throngs of boys, often joined by their older brothers, lay in wait for Jewish children on their way to or from school. I read about such incidents in the Jewish newspapers. One newspaper reported that it was not street urchins or delinquents who were harassing Jewish children but rather "good, school-attending children" who came out to the street to beat us up after listening to the Sunday sermon in church. I also read of an incident which occurred close to our orphanage. The boys who beat up the Jewish children, used clubs and sticks with razor blades embedded in them. There was also a story about some Jewish stevedores and other strong workmen, members of the Bund, the organization of Yiddish speaking laborers, who had sent a pack of young miscreants running for their lives, almost without lifting a finger. So that everybody would know: We were not all weaklings.

Our counselors began walking us to school on Sundays. This helped, for if an adult was around, the harassment was less severe. Once we were even escorted by a policeman. That really put an end to the hectoring that Sunday and the following one, but then the policeman disappeared and the louts made our lives a misery again.

During the Friday night assembly, the Doctor told us that he intended to publish an appeal to Christian youth in several children's newspapers. He said that he would ask them to leave us alone and allow us to walk to school peacefully. He was going to explain that their actions humiliated the Jewish children and disgraced the Christian children.

"Do you think that will work?" cried Itcho. "We should go to school armed with sticks and clubs and beat them the minute they come near us!"

"I disagree," said the Doctor. "If you come with clubs, next Sunday they will come with knives. And then what will you bring? Canons?"

"Let's go to war!" cried little Nathan gleefully. He was a bit of a fool, our Nathan, or just childish.

"A civil war among children?" asked the Doctor sadly. I had inkling into what the Doctor was thinking, and I knew he thought that children were a nation unto themselves. I thought it would be fitting for him to declare, *Children of the world unite*. Just like the communists say, *Workers of world unite*.

"So you are going to ask them nicely not to hate? Do you think they'll just agree?" asked Itcho. He was angry because he was forced to restrain himself and suffer all the insults, the spitting and the snowball attacks.

"I hope that if I explain why this kind of behavior hurts them just as much as it hurts us, they will stop bothering you," said the Doctor. "There is no point in letting things deteriorate even further."

"At the orphanage," said Rosie, "we have a court of law which strives for justice and forgiveness and the punishments here are only *clauses*. We have to sign up in advance if we want to fight someone, and at least half the time, the fights never take place. But the minute we go outside, even just to school, we see that the real world doesn't work like that."

"Perhaps we shouldn't talk about this in front of the little ones," added Josek, "but the seniors who will be leaving at the end of the year will go out into the real world which is nothing like what we have here." Things weren't easy for Josek. He was scared of what would happen to him once he left the orphanage. Here he was a king, but outside, when they spit on him, what could he do? Lodge a complaint with the children's court? Sign up ahead to beat someone up? Not to mention how difficult it would be for him to find a job. It wasn't easy for anyone these days. How would he manage?

"It's like we live in a movie," said Itcho, who wanted to make Josek laugh or at least make him a little happier. When he didn't succeed, he added, "Or in a book," and looked at Hannah. The Doctor was sad. You could see that he was worried by what Josek and Rosie had said. It was a sad Saturday assembly.

In the afternoon I read an article in the *Little Review* about the Sunday bullying. The boy who wrote it was angry that he was being hassled especially because he had always felt as Polish as can be. His father had fought in the Polish army and had even received a medal. The boy wrote that he didn't look Jewish. He had no side-locks, he wasn't one of the Orthodox Jews, he didn't even know any Yiddish. And still, on the way to school on Sundays, they called him *Beilis*.

I asked the Doctor, "What is a Beilis?"

He did not understand my question, so I said, "Beilis. They curse us and call us Beilis, Beilis."

"It is a name," he said. "Menachem Mendel Beilis was..." and then he stopped and said, as if to himself, "Actually, Beilis' story demonstrates what blind bigotry is, and why it is so dangerous."

"Why? Who was he? What happened to him?"

The Doctor's eyes softened. "Janek, you have the soul of journalist," he said.

This was, of course, very flattering, but I wasn't sure I deserved it. True, I liked to read newspapers but that didn't make me a journalist.

As if reading my thoughts the Doctor asked, "Would you like to see if you could write for a newspaper?"

I nodded without thinking.

"So write a few words."

"What about?" I was insecure.

"Who Beilis was, what happened to him, where and when."

I fell silent. I knew nothing about this Beilis guy. I had no idea how and where to get hold of some information.

The Doctor said he would provide me with the address and phone number of a lawyer who knew the details of the Beilis Affair.

"Perhaps you saw him; he was one of our guests here on Hanukah. He is a member of the organization that helps Jewish orphans. I suggest you make an appointment and interview him about Beilis."

"And then?"

"Then you'll write a short article, not more than a page, about the Beilis Affair. Remember, a news article has to answer five questions – who, what, when, where, why. And also how."

"Without connecting it to Sunday's harassments?"

"Of course you should mention it, before or after elucidating the Beilis Affair."

And that was my first journalistic assignment.

22

Mr. Hirsch, the lawyer, had a grand and spacious office. I sat on a large leather sofa in the waiting room and looked around. Two elegant secretaries, one older, the other quite young, sat behind two heavy wooden desks. The younger one, with a dramatic wave in her hair and lips painted bright red, introduced herself as Bella, and offered me tea which she served in a cup and saucer with two butter cookies. I had never been in a place like this. True, I had been in an office before, at the Shelter and at the public infirmary, but those were rundown offices, cramped and ugly. Here, as Staszek would say, everything stank of money.

Slowly sipping my sweet tea and staring at the secretaries, I imagined I was a rich man seeking the advice of a lawyer about some contracts. But having no business sense or knowledge about contracts, I decided to imagine I was a journalist who had come to interview a lawyer who specialized in affairs similar to the one I was immersed in at the moment, the Beilis Affair, which was exactly who I was. True, I was a boy living in a home for orphans and abandoned children, but I was a journalist in the making, or, as the Doctor put it, a journalist in my soul, a journalist who had set out to discover who Beilis was and why his name had become a curse.

I took a new notebook out of my satchel. Miss Steffa had given it to me that morning because she knew I had an appointment with Mr. Hirsch. She handed me the notebook in her usual brisk manner, and managed to whisper, "Good luck Janek, my dear," before turning to Abrasha who was standing behind me, waiting shyly for his turn. He had lost his pen and ink again, for the second time that week. He knew Miss Steffa would be angry. Many children were afraid of her anger, but not me. Perhaps because Mira had said, she reminded her of our mother. I wish I knew why.

Mr. Hirsch emerged from his office and accompanied someone to the door. He was short and bald with thick eyebrows like two paint brushes. I recognized him from the Hanukah party, when he stood in the corner of the room, apart from the other guests, gazing into the distance. Now too, his look was far away even though he glanced in my direction and said, "Sorry to have kept you waiting, Mr. Wolf."

Until then, no adult had ever called me *Mr. Wolf*, and no one had ever apologized for making me wait. I replied, "That's alright," and thought what else I might add. In one of his articles the Doctor wrote that people tend to be stingy with their gratitude, and in any case there wasn't much more I could say other than *thank you*, so I added, "And thank you for agreeing to see me."

Bella, the younger secretary, lifted her head. "Such a nice well-mannered boy," she murmured. "Tell your mother that I would be proud of you if I were her!" I thought that was nice of her, but Mr. Hirsch thought otherwise. Without raising his voice, but with a touch of anger, he said, "Unfortunately, Mr. Wolf will not be able to deliver the message, simply because he has no mother."

The older secretary didn't stop typing even for one moment and the expression on her face did not change. But Bella was distraught. "Oh, I'm so sorry," she apologized and bit her lip. "I had no idea."

"How could you know? It's not written on his forehead," Hirsch barked at her. "Had you kept yourself up to date with my diary you would have seen that he is from Korczak's orphanage." He was using me to chastise her.

She was on the brink of tears. "It's not every day that children come here," he addressed the room, as if a jury was assembled in front of him, "but if a child of Korczak's asks to see me I immediately arrange to have time for him."

The older secretary handed Bella a handkerchief and Hirsch led me into his room. There, seated in a comfortable armchair, I listened to the terrible story of Menachem Mendel Beilis. It had taken place 24 years earlier on the outskirts of Kiev in Russia – in the days when most of Poland was under Russian rule.

Beilis, a Jew who worked in a small brick factory, was charged with the murder of a Christian boy named Andrei. Eight days after the boy had disappeared, his body was found in a cave near the brick factory, riddled with multiple stab wounds. The police and the prosecution claimed that Beilis used Andrei's blood to prepare *Matza bread* for Passover.

Hirsch told me that an investigation, conducted years after the trial, uncovered the fact that the police had found out the identity of the murderer fairly quickly, but orders had come down from above to find or rather fabricate evidence which would implicate Beilis. High-ranking government officials, ministers, even the *Tsar* and his people intervened in the trial in an effort to prove that Beilis had murdered Andrei as part of Jewish religious ritual. He was accused of stabbing Andrei several times in order to drain his blood while he was still alive, meaning that the boy had died suffering intense pain.

The telephone on Hirsch's desk rang. He apologized and lifted the receiver. "Is it urgent?" he asked, and agreed to take the call. I shook my hand which was stiff from writing almost every word that Hirsch had spoken, and then I jotted down a few notes, things I didn't want to forget. I shook my hand again and stared at the wall behind Hirsch. There were some framed diplomas, paintings and photographs, among them a photograph of Hirsch with the Doctor, Miss Steffa, and some other people standing at the entrance to the orphanage, perhaps when the place was first opened. Hirsch finished his phone call and turned to me.

"Why did the Russian authorities want to blame Beilis for the murder?" I asked.

"As far as they were concerned he could have been a Hirsch or a Wolf, as long as he was a Jew."

"But why?"

"Why?" he asked incredulously, then smiled as if he had just remembered that I was just a boy. "Hate and racism can serve the authorities very well," he explained. "When times are hard, economically, for example, it is easy for them to divert people's attention from the problems the authorities themselves created or were supposed to solve, and to unite them in the hatred of foreigners, Jews or other minorities. This is what is happening in Germany today. Actually it is also happening in Poland."

His words scared me. "I think that here things are not as bad as in Germany, are they? Hitler is not here!"

"For the time being," he said, and beneath his bushy eyebrows, his eyes took on that faraway look.

Bella knocked on the door and entered. She apologized for interrupting, but there were some important documents to be signed. She apologized again until Mr. Hirsch told her emphatically that her apology was accepted. Then, she apologized again for repeating herself so often. He took the pages from her hand and began studying them, and I noticed that between every two pages there was a colored page. Hirsch always signed the white page.

"Why are there colored pages between the white pages?" I asked even though it was none of my business.

Bells smiled. "These are carbon copies," she whispered so as not to anger Hirsch again. "They are covered with ink. When he signs the top page the ink on the carbon paper transfers his signature to the page underneath."

Hirsch returned the signed papers to Bella and resumed his story. He told me that Beilis sat in prison for two and a half terrible years awaiting trial, which was postponed again and again. It was not only a trial against Beilis, but against the Jewish people as a whole, justifying the persecution of the Jews, the legislation of laws against them, denying them their rights, and using the hatred against them to strengthen the regime.

He took a large folder from a bookshelf and put it on the table. There, among the newspaper clippings, I saw a photograph of Beilis. He looked like any other Orthodox Jew, with a beard and a slightly bulbous nose. Had I met him on the street I wouldn't have remembered his face. There was also a caricature: His nose was drawn in grotesque proportions, his eyes were close together, cruel and cunning and his thick lips were curled lasciviously. He looked like a ravenous wolf. I had seen such caricatures of Jews before. In them, we looked ugly, nasty and greedy.

"But why did they blame Beilis, of all people?" I asked. "Was there any evidence against him?"

"The body was found near the small factory in which he worked, and they had a witness, a lamp-lighter, who said he had seen Beilis chase away two urchins from the factory yard, Andrei and his friend Zhania."

"And that was enough to indict him?"

"Beilis was a scapegoat; the intention was to prove that Judaism itself was to blame."

Hirsch continued his story and told me that the experts for the prosecution – clerics and scientists – could not prove the accusation of blood libel or that it was written in the Jewish holy books that the recipe for *Matza bread* calls for Christian blood. Beilis was acquitted, in part, thanks to a journalist who investigated the matter, and discovered that it was Zhania's mother who had committed the murder. She was a member of a criminal gang.

It turned out that on the day of the murder the two boys had quarreled. Zhania said he would tell on Andrei that he had played hooky from school, and Andrei threatened to tell on Zhania's mother that she was keeping stolen goods in her house. Soon afterwards they made up and were friends again. But when Zhania told his mother about the quarrel, she demanded him to bring Andrei to their home immediately. Apparently, it wasn't difficult to persuade Andrei, because he did as he was asked, and surely did not suspect what was about to happen to him. The two friends arrived together, but Zhania's mother wouldn't let her son in. She only let Andrei in, and that's when she killed him.

After Beilis was released he couldn't quite manage to recover from the ordeal. He immigrated to Palestine but did not fit in, so he sailed to America. Hirsch said he had died in New York a year earlier.

I was shocked by the story, not only because Beilis was falsely accused. I knew that things like that had happened before and would happen again. I don't remember much from the two visits to my father in prison, but do I remember him telling Mira and me that he had been framed. Mira was not sure he was telling the truth. She thought that perhaps he was trying to curry favor with us. Grandma used to say that all criminals claim to be innocent especially when talking to their children. Anyway, what I meant to say was that there are always false accusations and unjust trials, but this was about murder, not just burglary as in my father's case. Beilis was accused of bleeding and torturing the boy just so he could make bread. Even worse, this accusation was used to inflame hatred against a whole people, to humiliate them, persecute them, beat them, even kill them just because they, like Beilis, were Jews. And even though this wretched episode had happened more than 20 years earlier, we were still being cursed using his name. Beilis is a terrible curse.

23

The meeting with Hirsch came to an end. I now had enough information to write a one-page story, but I wanted to know more. Most of all I wanted to read the huge file on Hirsch's shelf labeled *Beilis in the eye of the media*. It contained numerous newspaper clippings, mostly in Russian but also in Polish, Hebrew and Yiddish. I couldn't read Hebrew or Russian, but what was there in Polish and Yiddish was certainly enough.

It was getting late and it was time I returned to the orphanage. Hirsch said I could come by any time I wanted, even without making an appointment. He told the secretaries to let me read the file. He also said that if I had any questions I could leave them for him in writing.

I was back at the orphanage before supper. A few of the younger children were dancing in the big hall. The Doctor was dancing with them. He took small dainty steps as if he were weightless. The children sang in Yiddish, and even though he did not know the language he mouthed the words and hummed the tune. When he spotted me from the corner of his eye, he left the small circle and asked me how the meeting had gone.

"Do you know why Hirsch suggested you return to study the file and prepare questions for him?"

"Because of you," I replied.

"I don't think so."

"Yes," I insisted. "He made time for me because I came from your orphanage. He even said so to his secretaries."

"Okay, okay," said the Doctor, "but I believe there's another reason."

We remained silent.

"He understood what sort of journalist you are," he finally said. "He realized that you want to learn more and more, that you delve into things, that you want to see the whole picture. A lawyer can appreciate the qualities of a good investigator."

Inside I glowed with pride, but all I said was, "I don't think the article will be ready for next Saturday's newspaper. Is that alright?"

"Yes, of course," answered the Doctor. "I'm sorry to say that this affair will never become outdated."

The children in the circle looked at him, and one of the girls stretched out her arm. The circle could not hold without him. Before going back to them he told me, "I'm proud of you, son."

I felt as if I would float away with joy. But a second later I was overcome with fear. I had not yet written a single word. Only part of the_assignment had been completed, the easy part. And what if I didn't succeed in writing the Beilis story in an interesting manner? Now I was afraid of disappointing everyone. My article had to be excellent! But why shouldn't it be?

During the following days my head was full of lead sentences, closing sentences, and some sentences for the middle. I even dreamt of the story, sometimes in pictures and sometimes in written sentences. In school I thought only about Beilis and the article I would write.

"Janek, may I know where you are at this moment?" the history teacher yelled at me. It took me a while to realize she was addressing me, because there were giggles all around. Everyone was looking at me.

"In Kiev, 25 years ago." I knew how idiotic that sounded. I couldn't believe that that was my reply.

The class roared with laughter.

"I am surprised at you, Janek!" The teacher was angry and tried to return to the lesson, but the class wouldn't let her. Someone asked, "Why in Kiev?" and someone else shouted, "Invite me to your time machine!"

"Quiet!" shouted the teacher.

Had she been our form teacher everyone would have shut up immediately. We were all scared of him, but this teacher didn't frighten us. She was pleasant, never hit us or hurt our feelings. She always spoke softly and couldn't quite make us pay attention. The Doctor also spoke softly, but he had a way about him, the words he used and his melodious voice always captured our attention and made us eager to hear more. The history teacher lacked this quality. I thought she was quite nice, not always very interesting, but we had teachers that were more boring than her, our form teacher, for example.

The previous history lesson had interested me very much. It was about life in Poland under the rule of the Russian Tsar. She explained how teaching, reading and writing in Polish were forbidden and that everyone was forced to communicate only in Russian. Schools couldn't teach about Polish heroes or Polish culture. Then, she told us about the *Flying University*, a group of youngsters and grown-ups who studied, in secret, behind closed doors, what the Russians forbade the Poles to know. That was interesting, but now, Beilis took over. I had no idea what the lesson was about, or what she wanted from me. The pandemonium in the classroom grew worse.

"I was just thinking about Menachem Mendel Beilis," I began explaining, but the noise and laughter only increased, and I couldn't continue. The teacher looked at me as though I had suddenly turned from an excellent student into a flippant troublemaker. She put her hands on her hips and screamed, "Janek!" But before she could add a single word, a big paper flower flew across the room, hit her chest and fell to the floor. She picked it up and looked at the petals opening like a rose. Now the class was absolutely quiet.

"Sorry, teacher," Itcho smiled at her. "I didn't mean for it to hit you."

She didn't know what to do. On the one hand, Itcho had thrown at her a sheet of paper, torn from a notebook. On the other hand, it was a flower – a very impressive flower, a real work of art.

The class remained quiet.

She thought for a moment then announced Itcho's punishment: to copy five pages from the history book 20 times, "and," she added, "it has to be in your own handwriting, I shall go over every page to make sure no one helped you. Don't you dare come to school tomorrow without 100 written pages." Then she asked us all to open our books on page 19, and told me to read out aloud until the end of the lesson.

On the way home, we talked about Itcho's punishment. To copy – that wasn't difficult, not like reading or writing. He could easily do that, five times, even ten. But 20 times? That was too much. A hundred pages by tomorrow morning? What should we do?

At a certain point Rosie and Hannah joined us. Rosie had heard what had happened in our class, and asked Itcho, "What exactly did you throw at the teacher?"

"Just a page from my notebook," Itcho replied. And I – just because I was so grateful for what he had done – said, "What do you mean, *Just a page*? A flower made of folded paper. Never in her life has she received such a flower, not even from an admirer, a flower even more beautiful than a real one!"

Rosie and Hannah looked at each other, "Like a rose?" asked Hannah and blushed. Only then did I realize what I had done.

"No, not at all!" I answered resolutely, but it was too late.

Itcho's face hardened to a scowl. I had revealed his secret. And I had promised him not to! That even under torture I would never tell anyone that he was the one who made a flower out of folded paper and left it for one of the girls on her bed. I didn't know at the time that it was Hannah, neither did she. Now the secret was out.

Rosie and Hannah intertwined their arms and walked away hurriedly. I looked at Itcho and started to mumble an apology. But he silenced me with a curse in Yiddish: That my intestines should be strung between two posts like laundry lines, and that the washing should be hung on them to dry, or something like that – and started running ahead. I lingered behind. I felt terrible. Itcho threw the flower at the teacher in order to divert her attention from me and for that friendly gesture he had been punished. Twice. Not only had the teacher given him that ridiculous assignment to copy all those pages, but I had inadvertently revealed to Hannah that he loved her. I wished I could undo what I had done, or at least have a good run.

24

When I used to run, my head would empty of nagging thoughts and I wouldn't argue with myself. This would happen not only while I was running but also afterwards. It would take some time for my head to get all mixed up again. Now, when I concentrated on something – like a newspaper or even homework – I could sometimes empty my head of any thought that wasn't connected to the subject at hand. Almost like when I was running.

That's why I wanted to immerse myself in the Beilis file. I didn't want to think again and again about how I had betrayed Itcho after he had acted like a true friend. I couldn't help him with his assignment; the teacher said she would check the handwriting, and mine was totally different from his. And as for Hannah, anything I would have said would only have made things worse. In any case, he stopped talking to me and refused to answer my questions. He just sat in the quiet room and started copying the history book. Even the Doctor thought the punishment was silly, but said that there was nothing to do but try to copy as many pages as possible.

I got permission to go to Hirsch's office. He was busy with meetings outside the office and the elderly secretary was absent that day. Bella, the young secretary with the wave in her hair and the lipstick, was there all by herself. She offered me a seat beside her, served me sweet tea and cookies, and gave me the Beilis file. I sat at the elderly secretary's desk, next to her black typewriter, heavy telephone and orderly pile of paper with three beautiful pens on it, and began reading. Soon, like during a good run, I was lost to the world.

I found some interesting facts, some of which Hirsch had told me and others he hadn't mentioned. For instance, I read that the prosecution claimed that the murder was part of a religious ritual; that Andrei had been stabbed 13 times and that number was sacred to the Jews. Not that it proved anything, but the police investigation found that Andrei had been stabbed 49 times. In response, the prosecution said, 49 is seven times seven, which is also a sacred number for the Jews, the number of days in the week. I know it's hard to believe that the court could accept such poor arguments as a proof of a murder, but that's how it was.

When the Tsarist regime fell and Russia became communist, all of the lies and the police's efforts to frame Beilis were made public. The lamp lighter confessed that he had been told exactly what to say in court, and was even given a bottle of alcohol in return. I read that immediately after the communists entered Kiev, they executed Zhania's mother.

I searched for articles about Zhania and Andrei, but couldn't find any. I only found out that when the prosecution was finally asked to talk to Zhania, it was discovered that he had unexpectedly died.

What is the meaning of *unexpectedly*? Perhaps some of his mother's friends did away with him so that he wouldn't talk and betray them? What was on Zhania's mind? What did he imagine was happening to Andrei inside his house the day of the murder? What did he think? That his mother and her friends were warning him not to talk, scaring him a little?

Surely, he had no idea that his mother could do a thing like that: kill someone; no, kill his best friend. Surely, he must have regretted that he had brought Andrei to his house, to his death. And after Andrei was killed, what did he think then? What did he feel? He must have blamed himself. When he heard that Beilis was thrown in jail and that the Jews were suffering because of a false accusation, what did he feel then? Perhaps he wanted to go to the police and tell them who really killed his friend?

The smell of sausage and mustard filled the office and distracted me from wondering about the two friends, Zhania and Andrei. Bella offered to share her sandwich with me. She was in a good mood. "It's fun in the office when Hirsch is not here," she said and reapplied her lipstick which had smeared across her mouth because of the sandwich. I couldn't refuse half a sandwich but I didn't want to stop working.

I jotted down some notes and quotes from the newspaper articles while chewing on my sandwich. The secretary spoke on the phone. Suddenly, I came across a short article which had been written long ago, shortly after Beilis had left for Palestine. It was well written, giving only the essentials, and cleverly worded. Every paragraph ended with a punch line, like a bash to the belly. I wanted to copy the whole article and present it to the orphanage newspaper in my handwriting. The article had been published a long time ago. Who would know that I didn't write it myself? How had I not thought of this before? I could have saved myself all the worry and stress. I didn't have to write the article myself and hope for the best. I could just copy, even from several articles.

The idea shocked me. I closed the file immediately and gave it back to Bella. I didn't want to be tempted. I wasn't a thief anymore.

"Sweetie, you can return the file to the bookshelf in Hirsch's room," said Bella, noticing me standing in front of her with the file in my hand. She was still on the phone but not about work matters, perhaps about love.

When I returned the file to its place, I noticed a stack of carbon paper on the bottom shelf, beside some other office equipment. Perfect! A quick thought flashed through my head. Thief or not thief, I grabbed the whole pile. Bella was still busy on the phone, I said good-bye, thanked her and left as fast as I could.

At the entrance I ran into Hirsch. He was just returning to his office. He was in a good mood, as though he had won a case in court. He asked if I had found anything interesting in the file, whether I had any questions, and if I wanted to continue our conversation.

"Yes, I've found all I needed," I replied without looking into his eyes. "I have no questions. I have to go." And I just ran away.

When I got to the tram station I was puffing as though I had run a marathon. I was pleased I had found the solution for Itcho's problem, because of the carbon paper he would have to copy only half the number of pages. When he sees what these papers can do he will be so pleased that he'll surely forgive me. That was important to me. Most important. Itcho was my best friend. But I could imagine the phone call between Hirsch and the Doctor, how the expression on the Doctor's face would change when he would hear that I had stolen from Hirsch. He would be so disappointed, he had trusted me, said he was proud of me, he had called me *son*. Now he would think I was just a liar and a traitor.

I didn't know what to do: take the stack of carbon papers to Itcho or return it to the lawyer's office. I felt like bursting into tears, like screaming or tearing up the papers and scattering them with the wind, and then just disappearing. I would never return to the orphanage, or go anywhere else. I tried to calm down. I counted 33 carbon papers and then I tried to think logically: For Hirsch these papers were of no importance. He makes a lot of money. Tomorrow he'll send the secretary to buy another stack. Ah, the secretary. Perhaps he'll blame Bella for not noticing that I had stolen the stack. Perhaps he'll fire her because of me. And after she gave me cookies and half her sandwich. But why should he fire her? And what does any of this have to do with cookies and half a sandwich? Besides, perhaps he had already fired her when he entered the office and saw her chatting on the phone? In any case, he's not happy with her, and she isn't happy there either. She should find another, less stressful job, or a husband, like Mira did.

Oh, why did I have to think of Mira now?

And the Doctor!? I'll explain to him that this is not a theft but a loan. I will give it back to Hirsch. I'll do extra duties and earn enough money to buy a package of carbon paper, even two, a gift from me to Hirsch. I took the carbon paper for friendship's sake, he'll understand, won't he? Maybe, but if he had had any idea I would steal anything, no matter what, he wouldn't have sent me to Hirsch. Besides, Hirsch is a benefactor of the orphanage. Because of people like him the orphanage exists. Perhaps now the lawyer will refuse to support the orphanage. Perhaps he'll convince the other benefactors that the Doctor has failed. It's a fact, the Doctor sent a thief to his office. Hang on, a thief? What had I taken? A few carbon papers? I had no choice, I needed them until tomorrow, and had I waited until I returned to the orphanage to get some money, all the shops would have been closed.

The tram arrived, but I didn't board it. Another tram came and went, and again I did not get on. I stayed there, wishing, the Doctor had not suggested I write about Beilis for the newspaper, and then I wouldn't have become so absorbed by the Beilis Affair, I would have listened to the history teacher and I wouldn't be so worried about writing a great article. I wished nothing had happened: That I had never come to the orphanage, that my leg had not been broken, that I hadn't been sent to the Shelter, that Mira hadn't married Staszek, that the nice lady hadn't fired her. What would Mira have done in my place? She would have returned the carbon paper. Mira would never have taken it in the first place. She would never take the chance of being called a thief.

Suddenly, like a miracle, the words the Doctor had given me when I had just arrived at the orphanage flashed through my mind: "Here, there is no reason to steal. If you need something, just ask for it. If it's possible, you'll get it, if not, then not." I immediately calmed down and knew what I had to do. Just ask. I know this sounds simple, self evident, but I wasn't used to straightforward solutions. Until that moment, asking for something wasn't an option. If I wanted something I either stole it or was angry I didn't get it.

I went back to the office. Bella was typing and I went straight to Hirsch's room. I knocked on the door, opened it, apologized for interrupting and asked if I could have some carbon papers. I waved them in front of his face so that he'd know what I was talking about and not ask too many questions. I explained that I needed them urgently, but that I would return the 33 carbon papers I held in my hand very soon. He looked at me with his far-away gaze as though he did not see me or was looking straight through me, and said, "No need, just leave two or three so we have some, until we can buy more tomorrow morning."

As I left the office my heart leapt with joy. I even tried to jump.

25

Now I had to convince Itcho to pay attention to me and my carbon papers. It wasn't easy. He was so stubborn. I sat down next to him in the quiet room. He had been there for several hours, copying from the history book or cursing, and imitating the history teacher. At first, he just ignored me and told me to shut up. The Photographer, who had been studying for an exam in another corner of the room, got up and came over. He took a piece of carbon paper, put it between two sheets of white paper and wrote, "Leica is the best camera in the world." I understood that he was no longer dreaming of the Retina; that he had fallen in love with another camera, but said nothing. Since the incident in the camera shop the Photographer and I tried to stay out of each other's way. What a pity. I think that if we hadn't stopped at that camera shop that Saturday afternoon we could have been friends.

The Photographer spread the two white sheets of paper on the table so that Itcho could see what the carbon paper could do. Itcho immediately realized how I had come to his rescue. He looked at me and then at the stack of carbon papers.

"There are 30 pages here," I said. He calculated quickly. That would give him 60 pages, and he had already copied 25. He started laughing with joy. We knew that the teacher, even if she realized that

Itcho had been helped by carbon paper, wouldn't say a word. The punishment she had given him was too severe, but she was not a bad person. She had probably regretted her decision by now.

When I left the quiet room Miss Steffa called me. She was standing in the hallway next to the Doctor, and both looked worried, even angry. Hirsch had probably called to say that I had asked for the carbon paper, I thought to myself. Or perhaps they were angry that I had found a way to reduce Itcho's punishment. And indeed they were cross with me, but it had nothing to do with the carbon paper.

As I approached them Miss Steffa shot at me, "Since you arrived here, you haven't once visited Mira!"

"Perhaps there's some misunderstanding," said the Doctor, looking at me hesitantly.

"No, there's no misunderstanding. I haven't been to see her."

"She came here while you were at Mr. Hirsch's," Miss Steffa continued. "When she heard that you were not here she wanted to wait for you, but I didn't let her." Turning to the Doctor, she added apologetically, "I can't allow family members to come here, what would the children who have no one to visit them say?"

I looked down at my feet. From above, you couldn't tell that one heel was taller than the other.

"Janek?" said the Doctor. There was no softness in his voice.

Miss Steffa scolded, "You should be ashamed of yourself. Your sister couldn't stop crying. You lied to us!"

Now I understood why everyone was afraid of Miss Steffa. Her anger was dreadful.

"That's not true. I am not a liar!"

"We gave you money for the tram almost every Saturday. We thought you were going to visit her."

"Where did you go on Saturdays?" asked the Doctor.

I told them the truth, "Sometimes I went to the movies, often to the Vistula River, just to look at it, or to buy a hot dog, or a special newspaper. Once, I almost went to visit her."

"*Almost* is not good enough," interjected Steffa. "That's stealing!"

"Not true, not true," I cried. "You *gave* me the money for the tram."

"Exactly!" she said without raising her voice. "That money was meant for travelling expenses to visit relatives. When you used it for other purposes you stole from the communal cash box."

I didn't want to speak with her any longer, so I turned to the Doctor. "You said I was a free person with the right to choose. So I chose not to visit Mira."

"What a pity," was all he said.

Two children were beating each other up. The Doctor allowed children to fight but only if they were matched in strength and as long as they did not hit each other in the face or bellies. Now there was a discrepancy between the opponents in size and in age, so he left us and went over to separate them. I stayed with Miss Steffa. She said, "Meet me at *the little shop* tomorrow. I want us to register for a trial."

"You are taking me to court for not visiting my sister?" I snapped at her.

"I can't force you to visit her – even though I think that it is ungrateful of you – so I am charging you with theft."

With theft, of all charges!

I wanted to ask Josek's advice. He was no longer my mentor, but I appreciated his opinion. The problem was how to get hold of him by himself, without Rosie. I didn't want to listen to her advice. At supper I slipped him a note, *I'm in trouble and want to talk to you. Alone.* When he read the note he immediately stopped joking with Hella, and became serious. After supper he went to fetch the key to *the little shop* so that we could talk there quietly. Only *fellows* and Yitzchak the painter, who used the room as his studio, were allowed to use the key to *the little shop*.

I told Josek what had happened. He sat on the edge of the table, folding his arms and stretching out his long legs.

"When they record the charge tomorrow, tell them you had no idea that what you did was a lie and a theft, and then apologize for what you have done. In addition, I suggest you offer to perform duties above and beyond what you are supposed to do, to earn enough money to return the sum you received for the tram fare to visit your sister."

"What's the point?"

"Think for yourself," he replied, and added, "in any case, that's what I would do." Again I thought how I used to call him *the righteous one*, scornfully of course. I remembered my grandmother saying about such self-righteous people, that they feel that they piss olive oil. I had to remind myself how good he had been to me during the previous trial, when I tried to steal the Retina, so as not to be cross with him.

"Hey," he drew me out of thoughts and back into the room. "You asked for my advice."

"Yes, I did."

Before leaving the room he smiled his lopsided smile and said, "When you offer to pay, you are taking responsibility for what you have done. You don't really think that it was okay to use the travelling money for other purposes, do you?" He didn't wait for a reply and ran off to his Rosie.

I was so agitated I could hardly talk to Itcho who was now beaming with joy, because he had managed, with the help of the carbon paper, to copy all the teacher had demanded.

I lay in bed and waited for the Doctor to make his rounds. I usually fell asleep before he came by, but tonight I made an effort to stay awake. When he finally entered the room and passed from bed to bed, listening to the breathing of the sleeping children and covering those whose blanket had fallen off, I was dead tired. When he reached my bed, I sat up.

"You've been waiting for me for a long time," he whispered and sat on the edge of my bed. I was so angry that I couldn't speak. We stayed silent for a while. And then he said, "I too, sometimes go to look at the river, I too like the Vistula. I have seen many famous rivers in other great cities, like the Thames in London and the Seine in Paris, but in my eyes the Vistula is the most beautiful river of all. Perhaps because the other rivers don't speak my language, I feel like a stranger on their banks. The Vistula runs in my blood."

He smiled shyly, perhaps because he had told me something personal. Then he whispered, "Janek, what did you want to talk to me about?"

"It's not important," I said and lay back in bed. Suddenly it seemed silly to complain about Miss Steffa or to insist that it is perfectly alright to use the tram money for something else.

"How is the article coming along?" he asked.

"I don't know how to write it yet," I sighed. I already had several sentences in my head but didn't know how to arrange them.

"Do you want some advice?"

I nodded.

"Don't get hung up on clever phrasing," he said. "Write as simply as possible, and as clearly as you can."

"Is that the way you write?" I asked unnecessarily, for now it was clear to me that it was exactly his style. Coming to think of it, I realized that everything he wrote, at least what I had read or what he had read aloud to us – was perfect. Yes, perfect, but not only because of its simplicity and clarity. There was something magical about it, something I could not explain.

"Good night Janek," he said.

"Good night, Doctor."

26

In the end there was no trial. Miss Steffa decided to withdraw her complaint against me. She accepted my proposal, actually Josek's proposal, that I repay the money by working, and immediately put me on kitchen and laundry duty. I hated working in the laundry, it was sheer drudgery. I would have preferred working somewhere else, in the yard, for example. It was the height of a warm spring and everything was green and the sun set later in the day. But I didn't complain. Miss Steffa said, "If you want to visit your sister, don't be shy, just say so and I'll give you tram fare."

In the past, whenever I saw Miss Steffa I would remember Mira saying that she looked like our mother. Now whenever I ran into her or heard her voice, my heart filled with anger. I remembered how she had sent Mira away, in tears. That really made me sad. So I stayed out of her way. I didn't want to be reminded of it, or of Mira.

On Saturday morning when the Doctor finished reading aloud the article I had written about Beilis, the quiet room ceased to be quiet. Everyone clapped. The Doctor looked at me with his kind eyes and smiled. I had tried to write as he suggested: simple and clear. I spent hours writing it. I worked hard so that what I had written would sound as though it had been easy to write. In short, the result was excellent! Itcho hugged me proudly as though I had been awarded a prize for investigative journalism.

Then the Doctor asked, "What do you think? Should we send the article to the *Little Review*, so that other children, Christians and Jews, can learn who Beilis was?"

"To the national paper?!" I asked in shock.

He smiled.

"Yes!" I shouted, and ran down to the kitchen to peel potatoes.

The following day the Doctor took me to the building where the *Daily Review*, the parent newspaper of the *Little Review*, was published. Everyone there seemed to be speaking on the phone, or rushing around or typing on typewriters. On the ground floor, two rooms had been allocated for the children's newspaper. In one of them, two boys and a girl were busy typing. Another girl with glasses was reading letters from a pile in front of her. She was the editorial coordinator, 16-year-old Malca. She explained that hundreds of letters arrived on the editor's desk every week, and that she read every one of them and wrote a summary in a notebook which she then passed on to the editor, who decided which letters would appear in the next edition of the newspaper and which would receive a written reply.

"Not a single letter is thrown into the waste paper basket," added the Doctor. "Every letter is given a proper attention, even if they are not all published."

I would have liked to read some of them, but didn't know if Malca would agree, and in any case the Doctor wanted to go to the other room, to see the editor. In the past, the Doctor himself had edited the newspaper but he could not do everything. So he delegated the editing to his secretary, Igor Newerly. Now Newerly shook my hand with surprising strength. Together we went down to the printing room. Some of the printers were former wards of the orphanage so they received the Doctor with warm hugs and pats on the back. One of them told the Doctor that he and his wife had just had a baby, a son. "Would you believe it," he laughed. "I, Shlemek the rebel, am a father!" He asked if the Doctor would come to examine the boy. The

Doctor agreed, and wrote the address in his diary. They made an appointment for the next day.

In the printing room there were trays with different sized block letters, with which the newspaper pages were prepared. The pages were then transferred to the large and noisy machines which printed them in thousands of copies. I watched as my first article was printed in a real newspaper, on the third page of four, under the headline: *Don't call me Beilis*. Below was the byline: *Janek Wolf, Warsaw, Guest Reporter*.

Wow!

I was given a few copies of the newspaper. One I wanted to send to Hirsch and the rest I would keep in the drawer of my bedside table, alongside a few newspaper clippings, such as President Pilsudski's obituary, and photographs and articles about the gold-medal winning runner Janusz Kusocinski, even though he had retired, and would surely not participate in the upcoming Olympic Games. I knew that my drawer would soon be filled with newspaper clippings about things that interested me, or articles I had written myself. I think mine was the most unusual drawer at the orphanage. I never locked it. What for?

The Doctor and I returned to the orphanage by foot. The newspaper's building was just a few blocks away. It was a warm day and a pleasant breeze was blowing. I asked the Doctor a million questions: How do guest reporters become regular reporters? ("You offer to write articles on various subjects, and when several of your articles have been published, Newerly decides whether to make you a regular reporter.") What is printed in the newspaper, is it exactly what the reporters wrote, or are changes made? ("Sometimes articles need to be edited or shortened. When a reporter is just starting out, his articles might require more editing, because it takes time to learn how to write for a newspaper. In time, when the reporter gains some experience, and develops a style of his own, there is less and less editing.") What does it mean to be an editor? ("To commission, arrange and correct articles, to decide what is important and what isn't, in every article and in the newspaper as a whole. The editor decides what should appear in every edition of the paper and what the newspaper should look like, its layout.") Who writes the headlines? ("Usually the editor, but the reporters can make their own suggestions.") Do reporters meet every now and then? ("Yes, they have regular editorial meetings. The newspaper has young reporters all over Poland; they talk to each other and help each other.") Don't they fight over subjects or steal ideas from each other? ("They are not supposed to. Stealing ideas is the worst kind of theft there is.")

We continued walking quietly, and then the Doctor said he liked writing articles for newspapers but enjoyed writing stories and books even more. Anyway, judging by all of my questions, he had come to the conclusion that he should write a brief set of guidelines for young reporters – a book which would answer all the questions I had asked, and several more, so that school children could get together and publish newspapers by themselves; newspapers which they would write and edit all by themselves, like the orphanage weekly, or like the national *Little Review*. He asked me what I thought were the most important attributes of a good journalist.

"Curiosity and investigative skills," I replied, because that was what he had said to me before he had dubbed me a *journalist in my soul*.

"And what else?"

"A sense of justice, and a desire to pursue the truth," I blurted out. I felt that I possessed these traits, and it felt good.

"Yes," he said. "And a caring heart."

I knew he said that because I had not visited Mira. I felt like a deflating balloon, pricked by a needle.

"That has nothing to do with journalism."

He remained silent.

"I can't forgive her."

"For what?"

I kept quiet for a moment, and then I repeated, "I just can't!"

He gave me a sharp look. "As you said yourself, you are a free person, you are free to choose."

I looked hard at the pavement. I didn't want to see the disappointment on his face.

27

Some people, none of them poor, have summer houses. Most of the time, these people live in the city, but during the holidays, especially during summer vacation, when they want to get away from the urban hustle and bustle and enjoy the beauty of nature, they leave the city for their summer houses in the countryside. We too, had a summer house, even though we were poor orphans. Every summer, all of us, a hundred and seven children, several tutors, Miss Steffa, the Doctor, the cook and the laundress, all left for the countryside, for a farm named Rozyczka. Our summer house was situated between wide meadows and a dense forest. There were separate dormitories for boys and girls with separate showers on the second floor, and a large dining hall and huge kitchen and balcony on the first floor. Two cows slept in the barn, and the farmer's wife taught anyone who wanted to learn how to milk them. We drank the milk of our very own cows.

I'm ashamed to admit that until the first summer at Korczak's orphanage, I had never left Warsaw, had never seen green pastures with wild flowers or a forest with tall trees. Never before had I breathed clean air or bathed in a river, walked in the fields or met a cow, except in the form of a meatball on a plate. All this happened to me at Rozyczka. We stayed there for the entire summer break, two whole months: no lessons, no homework, total freedom. We did whatever we wanted, we had fun. Sometimes we swam in the river, or walked in the cool dark forest where we picked immense quantities of wild berries, some of which we ate, and from the rest we made delicious jams which we took back to the city. The gloomy grey of Warsaw, to which we were accustomed, changed into green. In Rozyczka the world was green for us.

This perfect summer vacation also included our very own Olympics, which were modeled on the real games. The games committee which was a very important and respected children's committee, organized the races down to the minutest detail. During the first month the track was prepared and the participants trained for the events, and during the second month the races took place. For me the whole event looked tragic at first. Obviously, before my legs were broken, I could easily have won all of the running races, the 100 meter, the 200, the 400, and even the 800. Now I couldn't participate in any of them. Every time I exerted myself, jumping or walking a long distance, my leg hurt, running was out of the question.

Evil thoughts about Mira filled my head. Had she arranged to enroll me in Korczak's orphanage, without first sending me to the hostel, I would have arrived with my legs intact. The Doctor would have realized what a champion I was and sent me to train professionally, perhaps even with Janusz Kusocinski, Poland's champion runner. This was what he had done for other gifted children: the Photographer, Yitzchak the painter, and David the violinist, when he discovered their special talents. But now, what could I do except look at the athletes training: running, jumping, lifting weight... even barefoot! I was the only one there who never went barefoot. I felt like a starving man whose favorite food is dangled in front of his face, just out of reach; his mouth waters, but he knows he will never get to taste it. I was terribly jealous.

One morning, after we finished eating breakfast and were preparing to go outside, a farmer approached the house with a horse-drawn cart. He stopped at the entrance. The Doctor, who was sitting on a bench by the door, rose and walked towards him, smiling. After a few moments he called out, "Who will lend me a hand?"

The cart was full of sacks which had to be brought into the

kitchen. Nobody felt like working hard early in the morning, but still, the Doctor had asked. It was hard to refuse. The first to run to the cart was Josek, of course, then the Photographer and Itcho, and then other children, including little Nathan with his runny nose and side-locks tucked behind his ears. To tell the truth, I didn't want to carry heavy sacks, but I also didn't want the Doctor to think I was lazy. So I joined the others. So did Rosie.

"Come on girls," she called out. "Otherwise they'll say that all we're good for is picking flowers and sewing."

Sarah'le, who had sewn Itcho's costume for the Hanukah play, answered the call. So did Rachel, the editor of the orphanage weekly.

"Come on, Hannah'le," cried Rosie, but Hannah who was sitting in the shade of a tree, couldn't put down the book she was reading. She didn't even raise her head.

The girls and the younger children took small bags of flour and oats or baskets of eggs, and we, the bigger boys, loaded huge sacks of potatoes, onions, apples, plums and pears onto our backs and carried them into the kitchen. We felt we were strong men.

When we finished unloading the cart we left the kitchen and dispersed. Itcho stayed to talk to me for a few moments. He felt uncomfortable because he was training on the running track and I was walking around with a sour face, full of self pity.

He said, "I have a wonderful idea. You should sign up for mock Olympics. They have sack races, and egg and spoon races and three-legged races; you could hop on your good leg. It'll be fun!"

"Don't be a fool," I barked at him, since I took running very seriously. Given my illustrious past, jumping on one leg with an egg on a spoon in my mouth seemed totally ridiculous. I looked at a group of small children gathering around Hannah. She was still sitting under the tree, reading. "Hannah'le, read us a story," they cried in their whiny voices. "Please read to us." She refused. She was on vacation; she wanted to be left in peace.

Itcho poked an elbow into my ribs while looking at the scene before us. We immediately hurried towards them, imitating their whining, "Read to us, please, please, please..."

When she noticed us she blushed. In the end she consented, but only if Itcho and I agreed to stay. That suited me fine. I didn't know what to do with all the free time I had on my hands while the others were busy training for races and high jumps. Sitting there felt just right. True, there were some who were not interested in sports but they did not have an athletic past like mine. Also, unlike me, they knew how to keep themselves occupied and enjoy their free time, reading, playing musical instruments, dancing, or just messing around and lying on the warm grass. They did not miss running.

For Itcho, sitting there was also just right, especially because of Hannah. He loved listening to stories as he could not read on his own. The running races could wait, the race for Hannah's heart came first. Hannah put aside the book she was reading and opened another one. The little ones settled around her, and Itcho and I stretched out on the grass. We felt a pleasant ache in our backs from carrying the heavy sacks. We closed our eyes and listened to Hannah's hypnotizing voice as she read from a book by the Doctor, *When I Shall Be Small Again*. The main character was a teacher who did not like his drab life as an adult and wished he could be a child again. One day his dream comes true and he returns home to his parents and goes to school, and thus he remembers what fun it is to run and play but also how distressing it is for a child to be reprimanded by a strict teacher, or to be bullied by an older child, or to be upset because of a fight with a friend, or to be afraid of being punished.

Every time Hannah reached the end of a chapter and announced, "That's it for today," the children begged her to continue. Itcho and I joined them till she agreed. She came to the point in the book where the teacher, who had become a boy, has a conversation with his friend. They talk about how wonderful it would be if people had wings like the birds, so they could fly above the city or the forest, or perhaps only above the school, and when the wings grew tired they could switch to walking. They talked about the holes they would have to cut in their winter coats for the wings and how their sense of sight would improve thanks to all that flying. Something in the human brain would surely improve, because birds can fly long distances over continents without any guidance, no compass or map, and arrive exactly where they are supposed to. The children in the book were surprised that even though birds are smarter than men, it is mankind who rules the world. They understood that this has nothing to do with being smart. Perhaps man rules the world because he is a better killer than all the other animals. Man is a murderous animal.

This part gave me the shivers. I sat up.

"Enough for today!" declared Hannah and shut the book.

The children demanded more.

"I have been reading for hours," she complained. "If I continue I'll lose my voice! Go, run, play, you are children, not bookworms! Leave me alone. Let me read my book!"

Itcho told them that they shouldn't exaggerate and shooed them away by waving his arms. Before we left, Itcho thanked Hannah from the bottom of his heart.

"Come every day," she replied, and immediately blushed and dropped her eyes to her book which was waiting for her, open, on the green grass.

28

In the middle of the night, I suddenly felt a large hand covering my mouth so that I could not cry out. I opened my eyes in the dark and saw the moon shining through the open window. Josek was bending over me. He signaled to me to be quiet and handed me my shoes and clothes. I got dressed quietly and followed him downstairs. I had no idea what was going on but I saw a group of about ten boys and girls near the path leading into the forest. The Doctor was with them. When he took off his hat for a moment, his bald pate shone in the moonlight. Two more boys, Itcho and Little Nathan, came downstairs and joined the group.

"What's happening?" I whispered to Josek.

"The Doctor is taking us for a walk in the forest," he whispered back.

Had the Doctor not been there, I wouldn't have joined them. What do I care about the forest? And at night! I'm no coward but I'm not one to tempt fate, or wild animals.

"Why us?" I asked Itcho. I felt proud and thought that the others who were left behind asleep in their beds, would be very jealous when they heard what we did during the night.

"Don't you see? Everyone here helped unload the cart this morning. What a pity Hannah'le stayed with her book."

"Oh my," the Doctor cried suddenly. "What will we do if we're hungry?" and then with a mischievous smile he went with Nathan towards the house. Nathan slipped into the kitchen through the space between the bars on the window and quickly gathered a load of potatoes which he passed to the Doctor. Then he crawled out again, lifted his arms in a sign of victory and jumped to the ground. Who would have believed that Nathan could do such a thing? The potatoes were stuffed into two pillow cases and we were on our way. Josek led the way, a heavy pillowcase on his shoulder. The Doctor, holding Nathan's hand, brought up the rear. Around us the forest was pitch dark. Every now and then, our feet got entangled in the shrubs and pebbles underfoot. Good thing we had three flashlights with us. Weird noises of birds or small animals pierced the quiet. We had a strange feeling, festive, a little fearful, like before a great celebration or a calamity.

After a while, maybe half an hour or more, we arrived at a clearing in the forest. We collected some branches and lit a small fire and sat around it. Itcho sat to my right, Rachel to my left. She was a year older than me.

"I should have told you before," she said. " As the editor of the weekly newspaper, I have to say that your article on Beilis was excellent. I am not surprised that Newerly decided to publish it in the national newspaper."

I was pleased. It had been quite a while since anyone had mentioned Beilis or the article.

I suddenly realized that I had never spoken to Rachel before.

"The fact that we have never talked to each other before just proves how important our newspaper is," she said. "Look, 107 children in one house is a huge family. You can't really get to know everyone. The newspaper helps us to connect with each other, to find out what's happening with other people, what's bothering them, if they're scared or unhappy, what their plans are, what happened last week, and what to expect for the upcoming week. The newspaper helps bind us."

"I never thought of it that way," I admitted.

"Some children like listening to the Doctor when he reads

stories," she continued. "Others prefer listening to him read the orphanage newspaper. I obviously belong to the second group, because we are the ones who write it."

Rachel had a strange way of talking. Everything she said sounded as if it had been written and edited, ready to be printed in the newspaper. She told me about her work. In addition to commissioning articles, writing for the paper herself, deciding on headlines, devising new columns and sections and preparing layouts, she also had to choose what was worthy of publication from all the submissions she received as editor.

"That's the hard part," she sighed. "We get a lot of boring submissions. Like children writing about passing a test, or falling down and scratching their legs, or reminiscing about working in their father's carpentry shop. We're drowning in stuff like that and there's nothing we can do with it. But then many children, especially the younger ones, get upset that we don't publish what they've written."

"Why don't you ask the Doctor to explain in his editorial what is suitable for the newspaper and what isn't?"

She was silent for a minute and then said, "That might be a good idea."

We kept quiet for a while, and then she continued, "Janek, I know that you are not a member of the editorial board, and I wish you would fill out an application to join us, but in the meantime, would you be prepared to help us during the summer?"

"Sure. Gladly."

"Excellent," she said. "Many committee members are training for the Olympic Games."

I told her I was born to run and that was what I used to do until my legs were broken. Now, all I could do was watch from the sidelines, knowing that if I could still run, I would probably win many of the races. My self-pity didn't seem to move her.

She just said, "So fly with your words instead of run with your legs."

This advice sounded like a headline in a newspaper, the kind of headlines I liked.

I looked at the fire.

Josek began rolling the potatoes off the embers with a branch.

"Yulek," Rachel turned to a boy sitting next to us, and said, "Janek will help us with the newspaper. He is not taking part in the Olympics, so he has a lot of spare time."

Yulek smiled a small smile and then coughed.

When we returned from our excursion around three o'clock in the morning, we went to bed as quietly as possible and immediately fell asleep. We were woken at six by the shrieks of the cook, "Thieves, thieves, someone stole potatoes from my kitchen!" The Doctor had to explain that he was the thief. She cried that she would take him to court. We jumped out of bed and went downstairs. The Doctor defended himself and explained that he did not want to wake her in the middle of the night and did not want the children who joined him on his moonlight expedition to be hungry.

"You should have left me a note," she grumbled. "You know how afraid I am of burglars."

"You are right. I apologize."

She kissed him on his forehead and then shouted at us, "Why are you standing there in your pajamas? This is not a show."

We laughed and hurried upstairs to wash our faces and brush our teeth in ice-cold water. We got dressed and came down for breakfast. Everyone was talking about our nocturnal outing. Little Nathan seemed to have grown half a meter taller with pride. Again and again he told the story of how he squeezed through the bars of the window and how he passed the potatoes to the Doctor. Every time he told the story, the bars grew closer together and in later versions, they even had spikes. Josek told us that once real thieves had broken into the orphanage kitchen in Warsaw.

"There are bars there," I said.

"Yes, they were installed after that incident," he explained, and continued to tell us how the burglars entered through the windows in the cellar straight into the kitchen, and when they found no money they took the cutlery instead, because it was made of good metal which could be sold as is, or melted down and sold as scrap metal. In any case, they took everything and left quietly. No one saw or heard anything. But that same night they returned and threw everything they had stolen over the white wall into the backyard. In the morning it was full of strewn with knives, forks, spoons and teaspoons. The burglars probably didn't know that they had entered an orphanage, but as soon as they realized what they'd done, they returned everything. They were thieves, but they had a red line. From orphans they wouldn't steal, and if they did by mistake, they would return what they had taken. I wanted to think that my father was that kind of thief.

The following week the Doctor explained in his editorial why not everything submitted to the weekly is fit to print, and what should be sent to the newspaper and what shouldn't, just as I had suggested. That weekend I felt part of the weekly because I worked alongside the other members of the editorial board.

At the end of the Games, in addition to writing about the competition and the winners, I wrote some articles about the real Olympics, which were taking place at the very same time in Berlin, the capital of Nazi Germany. I based my reporting on the newspapers that Newerly had brought us from Warsaw.

I wrote mainly about the Black American athlete, Jessie Owens. He broke four world records, and won four gold medals, in the 100-meter race, the 200-meter race, the long jump and the relay race.

Hitler left the stadium so as not to shake the hand of a black athlete. He thought that Blacks were an inferior race just the way he thought of Jews. He hoped that the Olympic Games would prove the superiority of the Aryan race, but the black athletes beat the Germans again and again.

In one of the newspapers I found a photograph of Owens and the long jumper whom he had beaten, Carl Ludwig *Luz* Long, hugging each other. Owens said he won the long jump thanks to Long's advice. They became good friends.

29

Autumn came and a new school year began. The seniors had left, but Josek and the Photographer stayed on and moved into the tutors' quarters. Josek became a tutor, and prepared to immigrate to Palestine together with other members of a Zionist youth movement. The Photographer worked at the orphanage and also in a photography laboratory. In the evenings he studied professional photography.

Fifteen new orphans joined us, they reminded me of myself when I had first arrived, but we were also very different. They were younger than me and stuck together in one group. They seemed to feel less lonely than I had at the time, but I could be wrong. Some knew no Polish, only Yiddish, but in a few months they all spoke fluent Polish. Some of them cried at night, one of them hid bread rolls under his mattress for fear he would be hungry, and another covered his face when spoken to. He had probably often been slapped in the face. It took the new kids a long time to understand the rules. I felt I had come a long way from the time I was a new orphan. I was a now a *Resident*, (that was my status during my first three years in the home. It was only in the last status vote that I was promoted to a *fellow*).

The first time my name was picked out of the hat to serve as judge, I was reluctant to accept. I felt that I wasn't ready, wasn't the right person for it, because one of the defendants was the Doctor himself, and I happened to have seen him commit the offence he was charged with. On a cold afternoon – heavy snow fell outside, but inside it was warm and cozy – I left the quiet room where we were holding our weekly editorial board meeting (by that time I was already a member of the editorial board) and went in search of the Doctor. We wanted to hear his opinion about a new column that I had just proposed.

I walked into the great hall and saw him at the far end near the big book cabinets. I went over to him and then something very curious happened: the Doctor lifted Esterka – a little girl who sat next to me at the dinner table and whom I had never heard utter a word or seen look into anyone's eyes - and put her on top of the tall bookcase against the wall.

"Doctor, Doctor," screamed Esterka in her tiny voice, "I'm scared! Put me down!" He chuckled and took two steps backwards. There was silence in the room.

"Please put me down," she pleaded, on the verge of tears.

"I don't want to," said the Doctor with a mischievous tone in his voice.

I arrived at his side and he turned to me. "Yes, Janek?"

I was shocked by his behavior. Like everybody else in the room I looked from him to Esterka and back again. Even David, who was only interested in his violin, stopped playing and stared at Esterka who was stuck on top of the bookcase.

"Doctor, put me down. This isn't funny. I'm scared!" she whimpered, now in tears, her nose running. She wasn't a pretty girl, now even less so.

The Doctor turned to me again. "Yes, Janek, I'm listening."

The door to the quiet room opened and the members of the editorial board looked in to see what was going on.

"I have an idea for a new column," I mumbled and looked at Esterka. I had no idea why he was being so cruel to her. "We are in the middle of a meeting and we thought..."

"Yes?"

"If you don't put me down, I'll... I'll... I'll..." she threatened.

"You'll do what?" he asked her. "Take me to court?"

"Yes!" she said and wiped her nose with her hand. "I'll sue you. I don't care. If you don't put me down, I'll take you to court!"

"Really?" he asked her and turned to me again. "You want to hear my opinion about your suggestion for a new column? Tell me about it!"

He walked with me towards the quiet room and left Esterka on top of the bookcase, with everyone in the room watching.

"Yes, Doctor, I'll sue you!" she screamed at the top of her lungs.

When we reached the door leading from the great hall to the quiet room, the Doctor went back, lifted Esterka off the bookcase and joined our meeting.

We had a hard time talking to him after what he had done, especially because it was Esterka, one of the weaker children, who couldn't stand up for themselves, much less enjoy such a prank. But after a few moments we pulled ourselves together. I told him that I had thought of a column which would be called *what's the logic of ....?*

The idea was that anyone who didn't understand one of the house rules could send a letter to the editor, and we would check for him what was the logic behind the rule. If we found that something did not make sense, we might think of changing the rule, which we would suggest to the children's high committee and to the administration.

"Excellent!" the Doctor said and waited for Yulek to stop coughing. "Janek, you should write the first two questions yourself, and at the end of the column invite the children to send questions of their own."

The following day Esterka sued the Doctor. The complaint – together with the Doctor's odd explanation that he was just having a bit of fun – was posted on the notice board. The house was in turmoil. We talked of nothing else. We had heated discussions about whether Esterka should withdraw her complaint and forgive him – he was just having some fun with her – or whether there should be a trial, for he was obviously aware of the fact that she was suffering, sitting there on top of the bookcase. Many children, boys and girls alike, tried to convince her to withdraw her complaint. After all, the

Doctor had done so much for us, shouldn't we forgive him if once in a while he went overboard in a game. Esterka refused.

At the dinner table she sat in silence, her face flushed, hardly touching her food. I looked at her. She was one of those children who didn't seem to have the courage to breathe, let alone play or quarrel. Now, having sued the Doctor, she was the center of attention. This new situation didn't seem to please her, but at least she was present. Before, you hardly noticed her, as if she was transparent. Itcho suggested the Doctor himself ask her to withdraw her complaint. The Doctor refused. "Under no circumstances," he said.

On Friday night, before the Saturday evening meal, when the boy on duty passed around the hat from which slips of paper were drawn to decide who would be the judges for the coming week, I had no idea that this time it would be my turn. But that's what happened. I was told that once chosen, a judge could not shirk his duty. That was the rule, otherwise anyone who wanted to be liked by everybody and did not want to judge his friends wouldn't agree to serve. Okay, but why did *I* have to sit in judgment of the Doctor?

I said to Itcho, "I can't judge him! It isn't right!"

"Why?" asked Itcho.

"I... I admire him. I wish he were my father."

Itcho burst out laughing.

"What's so funny?"

"Everyone here wants him to be their father."

"Even I," Itcho added, "whose father isn't just anybody but the great comedian Schumacher..."

Since my trial for the theft of the Retina, I hadn't been to court again or had been chosen to sit as a judge. Both roles, defendant and judge, seemed dreadful to me. Now, in order to understand the system, I read the orphanage rule book and protocols of previous trials. I was as engrossed by the material as I had been by the Beilis case. On the first page of the book of rules was written: *If someone has done something wrong, it is best to forgive him*. This was followed by an explanation that thus the one concerned can learn to understand, improve and overcome his behavior in the future. Still, one cannot be forgiven for everything, especially as the court is duty-bound to protect the weak, the good, and the diligent. The court must seek to uphold law and order, because disorder is harmful to good and conscientious people. The book went on to say that the court as such does not embody truth and justice but that it is supposed to strive towards them, and that it is a great sin if a judge is knowingly disloyal to the truth.

I thought the Doctor was guilty. I saw how he had behaved, and his excuse, that he just wanted to have some fun, seemed lame to me. But I loved him, and Esterka – well, I hardly knew she existed until that incident. I felt it was unfair to expect me to judge him. How could I be impartial, if I was on his side?

I sat together with the four other judges at a table covered with a green baize cloth. The court clerk, Miss Steffa, read the complaints. All the pupils and tutors were present. Nobody wanted to miss the drama. That Saturday we had five trials to adjudicate. The Doctor's was the last. The first two complaints were trifle ones. A boy had stepped unintentionally on another boy in the shower, and a girl had used some thread which did not belong to her in the sewing room. In both cases, all the judges, including myself, did not hand down any clauses, just asked the boy to try not to step on anyone in the future, and the girl who took the thread to use only her own threads.

We continued. The next complaint was a tutor's who wrote that his pupil always returned late from visiting his family on the Saturday. Miss Steffa read what the boy had to say in his defense. He was late because he walked to his grandfather's house on Mila Street instead of going by tram. He gives the money he gets for the tram fare to his grandfather, who is poor and sick. I thought it was strange that I, who had used my tram fare to buy a hotdog and go to the movies with Itcho, should sit in judgment in this case. Miss Steffa asked each of the judges what clause we would like to hand down. We decided to acquit, but told him that on future visits he should leave his grandfather's house a little earlier, so as not to be late.

And then it was time to hear the Doctor's case. The atmosphere in the room was so tense; it could be cut with a knife. Everyone looked at us and at the Doctor and Esterka who sat up straight as a rod. The first judge handed down clause 100, the least harsh of the clauses, but not an acquittal. The second judge said clause 200, meaning the defendant did not behave properly and is warned not to repeat this behavior. I, the third judge, also said clause 100. The next judge chose to acquit and the last one chose clause 100. The bottom line was that the Doctor was found guilty in accordance with clause 100, but the court forgave him.

The judges stood up and the crowd dispersed. Esterka walked towards the exit. I was exhausted. I walked slowly towards the door. Just before I left the room I looked back. Suddenly, I saw the Doctor opening his arms wide and Esterka running towards him. They embraced and Esterka sobbed on his shoulder.

Only later did I understand what the Doctor had done. He had compelled Esterka to go to court against him, almost forced her, a child without any courage, to sue the man whom everyone wished was their father. He knew the children's court would find him guilty and that Esterka would be found in the right; that she would win the case. And that was exactly what he had wanted: that Esterka would become a winner.

30

My column *What's the logic of...?* was a great success. We received many questions and queries. For example: "Why can you only walk in one direction in the isles between the tables in the dining room?" The first isle is for walking back, in the direction of the elevator, the second is for walking forward in the direction of the library, and so on. (Miss Steffa's reply: "The one-way traffic rule in the dining room is meant to ensure that the children on duty serving meals don't collide with the children clearing tables and children sitting down to eat don't bump into those getting up from their seats.")

We also received the following question: "Why are there six brooms hanging at the entrance to the boys' and girls' dormitories?" (The Doctor's reply: "There are six brooms to make it easier for the children on duty to sweep the floors morning and evening, and they are also there as a sign of respect to an important work tool: why should we hide them away in a closet?")

Someone asked why there are marks for cleanliness, and the inquirer wrote: "The chart on the notice board shows that very few boys and girls receive a *very clean* mark. Most are *mediocre*, and there are many children, mainly boys, who are graded *dirty*. And if this derogatory mark weren't enough, the *dirty* children receive the most ragged clothes when new clothes are handed out." (Miss Steffa's reply:

"We do not mean to insult, simply to educate. And there is some logic to giving the better clothes to children who will take better care of them. Besides, we evaluate cleanliness four times a year and hand our evaluation to the children's committee so there are plenty of opportunities to improve. Those who advance from *dirty* to *mediocre* will soon receive better clothes, and if they continue to improve and are graded *very clean*, they'll be very pleased to see that when they outgrow their good clothes, they will be passed on to other children who will take good care of them.")

There was also an anonymous personal plea to the Doctor: "I see that you send some children postcards. Why don't you send them to all of us? I wait and wait, but nothing arrives."

I had received two postcards from the Doctor, one with a picture of the frozen Vistula River, in recognition of the fact that I got up early all winter and didn't dawdle in bed, under the warm blanket. The second postcard had a picture of a basket full of fruit and vegetables, in recognition of the cook's praise of my work in the kitchen. I kept the postcards in my private drawer.

When I handed the Doctor the letter, he sat down immediately to write a reply: "I don't send postcards on a whim. I send them to children who get up early all winter, to anyone who has been praised for his work in the laundry or kitchen, or who volunteers a lot, or to those children whose school grades have improved. In short, I send postcards to children who make an effort and their effort deserves to be recognized. Make an effort, I really want to send you a postcard!"

The Doctor was pleased with the column and the questions. He explained that because the rules and regulations are so familiar to him, it easy to forget that for some children, especially the new ones, the rules might seem arbitrary or illogical. Besides, he said, when he is asked to explain a rule, it gives him the opportunity to review it and see if it might be bettered. He praised me for the idea and on the Saturday that the column first appeared, he read it aloud. He was pleased with the column but I could see that he was sad. I knew that he had just been forced to resign from the board of a Christian orphanage he had run for years. And the radio station had decided not to renew his program *The Old Doctor*. He didn't mention any of

147

this, and not everyone was aware of his anguish. Those who were didn't want to bother him with meddlesome questions. Who knew understood that he had been dismissed because he was Jewish.

I continued to think up ideas for articles for the *Little Review*, but Newerly rejected all of them. "We've already published a story like that," he said about one idea, or: "We have regular reporters who cover that," or: "This is too complicated," and: "This won't pass the censor." Indeed, we were constantly wary of the state-sanctioned censors, who would disqualify stories from publication and force the newspaper to glue a white rectangle over an *offensive article*. They mainly found fault with criticism of the government.

I continued to ask permission to visit the newspaper every Thursday afternoon. Sometimes the Doctor accompanied me, other times I went by myself. Usually, I asked Malca, the editorial coordinator, to let me help her with the letters to the editor. Piles of letters were waiting for her on her desk and she was always glad of some help to record and sort them. Children from all over Poland sent questions or wrote to describe things that had happened to them or to their friends. Every now and then there was a letter from a parent or a teacher.

Sifting through the letters one afternoon, I imagined that Mira had sent a letter about me. I saw myself sitting next to Malca, both of us busy reading when suddenly, with a curious expression on her face, she hands me a letter she has just finished reading:

To the editor of Little Review:

Dear Sir, I am writing to you regarding the journalist who wrote an article about Menachem Mendel Beilis. His name is Janek Wolf, and he is my brother. I brought him up by myself, but, due to personal reasons I had to send him to Dr. Janusz Korczak's excellent orphanage. I assume he is in good health and happy. Would you please ask him to visit me on weekends as the other children do? I once visited the orphanage but Miss Steffa, the director, turned me away. I tried to explain that in all the time he had been there he hadn't once visited me. She promised to let him know that I had been there, but even after my visit he didn't come to see me. How can he do such a thing to his own sister who brought him up?

I imagined the harsh look in Malca's eyes as she waited for me to finish reading. And I imagined myself making all kinds of excuses, telling her about Staszek, about my legs, about the great athletic future that had been snatched from me, and Malca's look which did not soften but became distant and disapproving. I heard her angry questions: "Don't you care about her at all? She says here that she brought you up, is that true? Don't you know that poor girls have very few options? How could she have known what would happen to you at the Shelter? What did you expect her to do? Throw her husband out? And besides, she managed to find you a place at the Doctor's; do you know how many orphans are begging to go to a place like that? How heartless can you be?"

But all that never happened. No letter from Mira arrived at the newspaper. She probably hadn't read the article about Beilis, or for that matter any other articles, since I had stopped stealing newspapers. Also, it wasn't like her to write letters to the editor. Yet, in spite of all this, from the moment I imagined that letter, I looked for it on Malca's desk every Thursday.

I finally did go to see her, Mira I mean. Miss Steffa was ecstatic when I asked her for the tram fare. She even offered to accompany me, but I refused. I was tense enough as it was.

My stomach felt queasy as I rode the tram, and again when I read the signs posted everywhere, *Don't buy from Jews* and *Death to the Jews*. When I approached my old neighborhood I felt even queasier. I walked along slowly, greeting two old neighbors who were on their way to synagogue, but they didn't recognize me and didn't return my greeting. No matter. The hard part was still before me.

I stood in the stairwell for a while. As always, there was a strong smell of damp. At least in winter, there was no stench from the sewer pipes, like in the summertime, because it was so cold; something to be thankful for, I muttered to myself sarcastically, and knocked on the door. Staszek opened the door; he was really surprised to see me. For a few moments he just stood there in his dirty clothes and then shouted, "Janek, I hardly recognized you," and just to be funny, he added, "You almost look like a human-being." I had several replies to this joke on the tip of my tongue, like "Same to you!" but I remained silent. Shmulik, whom I hardly recognized, and a toddler with a runny nose, clung to Staszek's legs. I had no idea that they had had another child.

Staszek said, "Now that you've finally remembered to come, Mira's not here."

Suddenly I became frightened. I thought, perhaps she had died giving birth to this baby. "Where is she?" I managed to ask.

"In the hospital."

I couldn't utter a word. I was so scared for Mira.

He said, "She was sick, but the doctors say she'll be fine."

I smiled at Shmulik, he didn't smile back. He looked sad, perhaps because his mother had been away for quite a while and he missed her and was worried about her.

Staszek introduced me to the children. "This is your uncle, the famous Janek. Now make way, let him in."

He left the door open and I followed him in. I had forgotten how cold and bleak the small apartment was. It smelt of diapers and mildew. I was sorry I hadn't brought something for Shmulik who looked at me with his big eyes. The baby was crying and tears mixed with snot were smeared all over his face. Staszek tried to light the stove. "Want some tea?"

No. I just wanted to get out of there. "She'll be alright, won't she?"

"Yes, yes," he said, as if in despair, "And thanks for coming."

I cried all the way back to the orphanage. I didn't care that everyone on the tram could see me.

31

I meant to go back and visit Mira, of course I did, but I postponed my visit from one Saturday to the next, with a fresh excuse every time. Once I went to the movies with Itcho, another time I stayed home to prepare for an exam. One Saturday I joined the Doctor and some children who had no family to visit on weekends, for a trip to the zoo. Another Saturday I stayed home because two days earlier, during my weekly visit to *Little Review* the editor, Newerly, finally approved an idea I had for an article.

At first he cut me short, as usual. "No," he said. "We've already written about the *Ghetto Benches*. We've already interviewed Jewish students about how humiliating the new law is. It is appalling to have to sit on separate benches in the lecture halls just because you are a Jew."

"Yes, I know, but..."

He didn't give me a chance to explain and started walking away, saying, "Our newspaper, just like real life, is becoming more depressing from week to week."

I almost stopped him in his tracks. "But what I'm suggesting isn't depressing at all, and has never been written about in our paper, meaning in *Little Review*."

"Okay," he said and stopped. "Surprise me."

I smiled, for I knew that I had finally found a way to become part of the paper. I had no intention of suggesting subjects from adult newspapers, because for that Newerly had his regular reporters. From now on I would suggest new angles for stories that the newspaper was already reporting. That is just what I did with the *Ghetto Benches*. "I want to go to Warsaw University and find non-Jewish lecturers and students who objected to the segregation of Jewish students and interview them about it."

He raised his eyebrows. "Fine, and if you find even one lecturer or student who is willing to speak on record I'll be overjoyed!"

As it turned out, it wasn't easy at all to find lecturers or students who were willing to talk to me. I spent my afternoons walking along the paths and corridors of the university, usually by myself, sometimes accompanied by Yulek. I waited outside lecture halls to ask students what they thought about the *Ghetto Benches*.

Some didn't reply, others ridiculed me or answered rudely, and still others asked why did I care. Once somebody kicked Yulek, cursing, "You're here to spy for the communists, aren't you? You stinking Jew!"

Two weeks passed before I found an old man, a professor of history, who was willing to cooperate. He came out of the lecture hall, carrying a stack of heavy books under his arm. "It's a disgrace," he said as we walked side by side. He told me that at the start, he told his students to stand during the lecture in protest of the new law, but after a few weeks they complained that their feet hurt and sat down. That was the end of the protest.

"Do you know any other people at the university who would be willing to speak out against the *Ghetto Benches*?" I asked.

He invited me to sit in on his lecture. He stood at his lectern looking out at a hall full of students. The back benches, where the Jewish students were forced to sit, were painted yellow. He introduced me and asked who was opposed to the segregation of Jewish students from the non-Jewish ones in the lecture halls. Ten students raised their hands. When he asked who was in favor of segregation, 15 students raised their hands. When he asked who didn't care either way, 30 raised their hands.

When he asked who would be willing to protest, to demonstrate, by standing during lectures, one girl and one boy raised their hands. I interviewed them after the lecture. They said that the *Ghetto Benches* were racist, that the Jews were part of the Polish nation, that the government was racist and encouraged intolerance and hatred, fomenting hooliganism, in order to curry favor with neighboring Germany, things like that. As I wrote down what they said, the boy asked not to be mentioned by name, he was afraid to get involved.

"What could happen?" I asked. "This is a childrens' newspaper."

He sighed and explained, "Somebody could see this and decide to beat me up, or I could be expelled from university, even sent to prison. These days, it's dangerous to express a dissenting opinion."

At that moment I knew that Newerly was right. In the end, my article will also be depressing. My interviewees were a small and frightened minority. Most of the students just didn't care.

My article was printed on the front page of *Little Review* – a real honor – but no-one read it. Because the interviewees criticized government policy, the censor scrapped the whole thing. A white square was pasted on top of the article before the newspaper went to print.

"That's why we have to immigrate to Palestine," Josek said when I told him about my censored article. It was Sunday, and Josek was accompanying pupils to school.

"And this is another reason," he added pointing to some graffiti on a nearby wall: "*Hitler, come to Poland! Deal with them here, too.*"

"When are you leaving?" asked Rosie in anger.

"Soon," answered Josek. "As soon as I can. Won't you come with me to a youth movement meeting?"

She didn't want to. "It's not for me. All those dreams about a country with camels doesn't mean anything to me. I want to be a lawyer, not a farmer or sentinel."

"What will you do next year when you leave the orphanage?" he asked. "Won't you join me?"

"No," she replied. "I'll find a job and save up for university."

He remained silent.

"The Doctor will help me," she said. It was true. The Doctor often tried to help graduates to find jobs, writing recommendation letters, making phone calls, and appealing to his circle of associates and friends on their behalf.

Josek said, "There's a limit to what he can do for us now."

He stopped, and all of us stopped with him. Once again, we were audience to a heated argument.

"There were two pogroms this year," Josek shouted and stamped his foot. "Dozens of Jews were murdered, their houses set on fire and their shops looted. Here, in our country, in Poland. What else has to happen before you realize that there is no place for us here anymore?"

"That happened in faraway towns," she said. "Not here in Warsaw."

"And here there are no murders?" he continued shouting. "There is a new story every day. Ask Janek, he'll tell you what's in the newspapers."

I cleared my throat in embarrassment.

"Perhaps things aren't as bad as you think," said Rosie. "For example, the Doctor has been given a new radio program."

But this new program was very different from the previous one. It was not intended for children, and the Doctor spent much of his time on the air talking about the loneliness of children and adults.

A few months later, Josek went to Palestine. Before he left he gathered us all for a final talk. He was very enthusiastic about the Land of Israel, he talked as if he was already there, being very happy and waiting for us to join him. He said to me, "Janek, there are newspapers there, too, you know," and added in a loud voice so that Rosie could hear, "and it's never cold there like it is here."

"Yes," she mumbled. "It's as hot as hell."

At the end of the year she left the orphanage, and she did not join him.

32

We were now seniors. When the new pupils arrived at the end of the summer, Hannah and Itcho applied to the children's committee to become guardians. Both were accepted. They took care of their pupils, wrote remarks in their little notebooks, followed them around and explained things to them. Hannah even moved her bed next to that of one of her pupils because until she had come to the orphanage, the little girl had never slept alone. Hannah and Itcho organized a performance, they were reading aloud for all the little children. They were now together all the time. They went to movies on Saturdays and once even snuck into Schumacher's show. Sometimes I was jealous, because Hannah filled all of Itcho's heart, and not only she, but also his pupil and the Bund party which he had joined. Itcho loved the Yiddish workers' union. He had no time left for me. Rachel who had graduated from school, left the orphanage, and I took her place as the editor of the orphanage weekly. Yulek, Marek and Blumka who was two years younger than us, but wrote better than any of us, were my deputies.

That year, our last year at school, we had many exams. None of us had enough money to continue to high school, but still we tried to get good grades so that one day, if we wanted to, we'd be able to continue our education. I thought of studying journalism, but sometimes I thought of medicine, because of the Doctor. Hannah wanted to study literature and be a librarian, and Itcho didn't want to study at all. He wanted to find a job, something manual, where he could use his hands, and also dreamt of opening a Yiddish youth theatre.

While we were dreaming our dreams, thousands of Jewish refugees, who had been driven out of Germany, were interned in refugee camps in appalling conditions. I read about them in the newspapers and also about the possibility of Germany attacking Poland. I kept searching for ideas and angles for news articles. Newerly rejected almost all my suggestions but there was one he accepted with no hesitation: an interview with the Doctor about his childhood, about the wars and the hospitals and how he came to work with orphans. I told Newerly that the story of the Doctor's life would be of great interest to us, the children of the orphanage, but not only to us. I was sure that such an interview would be of great interest to many others, children and adults as well. Everyone knew the Doctor because of the books and stories he had written, because of the orphanages he ran and because of his radio programs.

Newerly said, "You're right, that could be very interesting. The Doctor is an unusual man who has led an unusual life."

For a moment I was full of enthusiasm, but then he predicted, "But he won't agree, I have asked him several times and he has always refused. You see, Dr. Korczak likes to publish his ideas about education or to write stories and books, plays and articles but when it comes to talking about himself he prefers not to."

"And if he agrees because it is me who asks him to?"

Newerly smiled. "If you succeed in getting an exclusive interview, not only will your interview be printed on the front page, but you'll also become a regular reporter."

"We have a deal!"

We shook hands on it.

I thought that my dream would at last come true, but the Doctor refused to be interviewed. I told him that if I delivered an interview with him, not only would it appear on the front page but I would be made a regular reporter. He smiled, "I would like to make you happy, to give you such a gift, but I don't feel comfortable being interviewed. I don't like talking about myself. I'm sorry."

I couldn't conceal my disappointment.

"Isn't the orphanage weekly enough?" he asked.

"It's not that it isn't enough, but I want to write about other things too, things that have nothing to do with our home."

"I understand," he said. "You're right, our weekly deals mainly with our children and the home. Why don't you think of a feature which brings the outside world into the home?"

I thought about it and after a few days I had an idea for a new column. I hadn't yet decided whether to call it *Life outside our Home*, or *A Letter Home*. In any case, I wanted to print a weekly letter from one of our graduates in which he or she would write about life outside, in the real world. I thought that a column like that, beyond the interest and the curiosity it would arouse, would also serve as encouragement and perhaps as good advice for all of us, especially the seniors who would be graduating at the end of the year and leaving the orphanage. I wanted the graduates to write about the rooms they rented, the jobs they found, the food they ate, the people they met; in short, what their life was as independent adults. While I was thinking about the new column and whom I might approach to write for it – other than Josek, who would write from Palestine – I looked out the window and saw Beautiful Rosie. She was sitting on a bench in the garden, with Hannah by her side. Rosie laid her head on Hannah's shoulder. Suddenly they stood up, embraced, and were about to part when Miss Steffa joined them. She handed Rosie a cloth sack full of apples and kissed her on the forehead.

I hurried towards the entrance door, almost bumping into Miss Steffa and Hannah who were just coming in. I ran into the yard calling, "Hey Rosie, wait a minute!"

She turned round. "How are things, Janek?" she asked, smiling a sad smile.

When I asked how she was she answered, "Move on to the next question."

I accompanied her to the gate, and on the way I told her about the new column. I asked if she was willing to write something for us.

She laughed a short and bitter laugh. "Are you asking about my law studies?"

I stared at her. I had no idea whether she was being sarcastic or serious.

She was being sarcastic. There were no studies for her. She had not been admitted to university. Her older brother had been arrested and imprisoned. She had found work as a seamstress assistant. She was earning enough to rent a small room together with three other girls. She said that in her neighborhood there were not many Jews, and that she was easily recognized as one because of her dark skin and hair. It didn't help that she was beautiful; people still harassed her. Blond, fare skinned Hannah would have it easier, she said, her eyes filling with tears.

"And what about Josek?" I whispered. "He is waiting for you in Palestine, for sure."

"I'm trying to go," she said in a choked voice. "I even joined his youth movement but it seems I was too late. The British have locked the gates of Palestine."

I knew what she was talking about. From what I read in the newspapers, I knew that the British had stopped issuing visas to Jews.

Suddenly I thought of what Hannah had said when we had had the mumps – that Rosie was always afraid things would go wrong for her.

"Hey Janek, find someone else to write for your column. I'm sure some graduates were more successful than I. At the moment I'm just not right for it. But things will change, won't they?"

"I'm sure things will improve," I said trying to sound convincing but in my heart I thought that indeed everything had gone wrong for her.

We reached the gate, and then I saw her. She was standing on the pavement, waiting for me, my sister.

33

I would have recognized Mira anywhere, but she didn't look like herself at all. It seemed like a million years had passed since we ran together in the streets on our way back from the rich lady's house. Mira used to look like a young girl, like the older sister of a little boy. Now she looked like a woman, like someone to whom you would say, *Excuse me, ma'am*, if you unintentionally bumped into her on the tram. Now, if someone saw us walking together on the street he would probably assume she was my mother. I looked at her, she looked tired, drained, and very serious, not like a cheerful girl who would suddenly burst out laughing in the middle of a racing spree.

I walked towards her and pointed at my feet to show her that I wasn't limping anymore. She smiled with her mouth closed and her eyes filled with tears. I looked away, because I remembered that crying, especially when Mira was crying, could be contagious.

"You know that I came to see you, don't you?" I asked. The smile disappeared from her face and I regretted I had mentioned it. I was ashamed that I had not been to see her since. I shuffled my feet and studied them carefully.

Mira came straight to the point. "Staszek's brother has arranged immigration papers to Palestine for us."

"How did he manage that? It is impossible now!" I declared. "The British aren't letting any Jews in!"

"True," she said. "Staszek's brother went to great lengths to get those papers."

"And he succeeded?" I could hardly believe that Staszek had such a clever brother, so clever that he could accomplish the impossible.

"That's what I've come to tell you."

I understood. She had come to say goodbye. She's going to Palestine and we'll never see each other again. I leaned against the wall and slid down till I sat on the pavement. She sat down next to me. Like me, she pulled her knees up to her chest. Our shoulders touched and we were almost the same height.

How could she do such a thing? She had promised Mother and Grandma that she would always take care of me, as if I were her child. She wouldn't leave Shmulik like that, that's for sure. I was getting angrier and angrier.

"When are you leaving?" I asked coldly.

"Next week. But listen, I told Staszek, 'Your brother has to take care of my brother, too. Without Janek we're not going anywhere. I was very serious. I said: 'If Janek can't come with us, I'm staying here with the children, I don't care what happens. You can go by yourself if you wish.' It wasn't easy for Staszek's brother to arrange for another permit but he managed it! You can come with us!"

A bird cried out in the distance.

"Did you hear what I said?" Mira asked.

All I managed to say was, "You were right, I really do feel at home here, at the orphanage."

Mira said, "They say that war is about to break out. Did you that they set Staszek's cart on fire? It's a miracle he's still alive."

I began stammering, "I really wanted to visit you, Mira... I know you had another baby... that you were sick..."

"Let it be, Janek," she put her hand on my leg. "I can't go and leave you here. You have to come with me. I am your family."

But now she is not my only family, I thought to myself. Just as her family has grown, so has mine. Now it includes people, who are closer to me than my biological family, the Doctor for example, and

Itcho, and Hannah, even Yulek. Our lives, Mira's and mine, had diverged long ago.

I wanted her to understand why I would not go with her but all I could manage was a jumble of disjointed sentences. "A while ago I was voted a *fellow*. I'm a senior now. Sometimes I publish articles in *Little Review*. I edit the orphanage weekly".

She didn't ask what a *fellow* was, what it meant to write for *Little Review* or edit the weekly newspaper. She didn't even say, as our grandmother would surely have said, 'The world could come to an end, and he wouldn't even sneeze'. She bit the nail on her thumb and said, "Yes, I know."

I looked at her. "You know?"

"I even read the article about Beilis. It was very interesting, Janek."

"What!? How?"

"Miss Steffa."

I was astounded.

"Yes," Mira nodded. "She visited me a few times."

I said, "She said she threw you out!" I felt my anger rising.

"Yes, and I was so surprised when she came over and brought me the newspaper with your article. She calmed me down; said you would surely come to see us, but till then she would come every now and then to let us know how you were doing and also to see how we were. Wasn't that nice of her?"

I couldn't reply I was so shocked. Why didn't Miss Steffa tell me that she was visiting my family? I had been so angry with her since that argument I couldn't look her in the eyes. Now I regretted it so much. I stood up and so did Mira, straightening her dress.

"You've got a few days to get ready; we're leaving on Tuesday morning."

"Look here," I said, then swallowed and cleared my throat. "I can't leave now. I've got final exams, I'm finishing school. I can't leave before the exams. And in the summer we are going to the farm. Two months in the country. Do you know how much fun it is? We've been waiting for it the whole year."

"And then what?" she asked.

"Then we'll see," I answered and looked away. "I belong here, just like everyone else." That's what Itcho always said when people talked about leaving Poland.

"Janek..." She came closer and put her arms around me like she used to do when I was really small, when I loved her like a mother.

I whispered, "Mira'le, I can't come with you."

She pushed me away and looked straight into my eyes. "Think about it for a day or two. Not longer. We have to buy tickets for the train and ship."

I wanted to beg her not to go, but I knew that was an irrational, unfair request. We were silent till Mira said she had to go. I wanted to delay her departure so I asked, "What's the baby's name?"

"Yakcov, Yankel, after Grandpa."

I too was named after Grandpa Jacob. Grandma used to say that he was an excellent person, that he had a good heart; he cared for people. But what did he do? Who was he? What kind of father was he to my mother? I knew nothing about him.

"Did you know him, our grandfather?" I asked.

"I'll tell you everything you want to know on the way to Palestine, on the boat."

"I'll come to say goodbye."

"I've got another baby on the way," she said before she left.

34

I hadn't seen her for a quite a while, but all the while I knew she wasn't far away, at least she was in the same city, 15 minutes by tram. I didn't want her to leave, certainly not forever. I kicked the wall and a terrible pain shot through my bad leg. I entered the house, and even though I walked normally I felt as if I was limping badly.

At night my sleep was as thin as cardboard, and my thoughts wandered all around Warsaw. I dreamt that Mira and I were racing each other towards home until she began laughing which slowed her pace. I woke up and thought again about Grandma's house and Korczak's house and about everything that had happened and everything that might still be in store for me.

I tossed and turned till I finally got up and went outside. I wanted to talk to him, to the Doctor. I climbed up to the attic. A light shone under the door, he was awake. I knocked, and heard a chair scraping the floor. He opened the door.

I told him that my sister had immigration papers to Palestine for the whole family, including me. He invited me in and motioned for me to sit on the small sofa. He sat down opposite me with his back to his desk.

He said, "In the past I didn't think that Palestine was the solution to the Jewish problem. I am a Pole, totally Polish. Now I'm beginning to think that it is the place for us Jews. We have no future here. Sadly I have to say that I too have to uproot myself and emigrate there. Perhaps I'll grow old in Jerusalem, write about Biblical heroes, about Moses, David and Saul when they were children."

"So why don't you do so?" I asked.

"Perhaps I'm too old to start afresh, in such a different environment, without my mother tongue; perhaps I cannot leave a hundred and seven children... Maybe, I'll emigrate with the children in a year or two, open an orphanage for needy children, Jews and Arabs..."

We were silent for a few moments, and then he said. "You've made the right decision, my son."

He called me *my son*.

I didn't argue with him, I didn't say, *No, no, I don't want to leave*. I didn't say, *my sister isn't my only family, I have all of you*. I didn't say, *the newspaper, final exams...the orphanage weekly... the summer holidays*. At that moment I knew the right choice was to leave now and go with Mira to the land of Israel. After a moment I thought how lucky I was to have Josek there, and what a pity that Itcho wasn't coming with me.

The Doctor said, "I'll miss you."

"Me too."

I asked for a final gift, and exclusive interview.

He was surprised. "But even if I agree, you won't become a regular reporter for *Little Review* because you won't be here anymore."

"I know, I don't even care if it's never published."

"Why then?" he asked.

I really couldn't explain, not even to myself. So I just said, "So that I'll know."

"This was my father's desk," he began in a quiet voice taking a sheet of paper and a pen out of the drawer. "He was a lawyer." The Doctor stood up and we switched places; now I was sitting at his father's desk, and he stretched out on the sofa.

"What would you like to know?" he asked.

I asked him what seemed to me most important, what kind of child had he been.

Not like us, not at all. Janusz Korczak, who was born Henryk

Goldszmit, grew up with a father and mother and sister in a spacious, beautiful apartment. They had plenty of money and he had toys and books and clothes and blankets and coats, and was never cold in winter. He was never hungry. Still he was a sad and pensive child who was easily hurt by an angry word, a perceived slight, a threat or frightening behavior. And even as a child, he used to look at poor children and feel sad that he was not allowed to play with them. The only one in the family who really understood him was his grandmother. He talked of her with love and longing. I too loved my Grandma.

The Doctor told me that as a boy, he had had a dream, to gather all the money in the world and throw it into the sea.

"Why?" I asked, a little shocked. I would never have thought of something like that.

"I saw that there were so many people without anything, and I understood that having money or not having money causes so many problems and difficulties, it leads to hatred, wars and death. I thought that if no one had any, there wouldn't be any problems and the differences between rich and poor would disappear."

His grandmother called him *my philosopher*. I would have called him *saint*, without being cynical. I already knew that had he wanted, he could have been a famous and wealthy pediatrician. But he had no real possessions of his own, only his father's desk.

When he was five, he had a canary, but it died. He wanted to bury it in the garden and put a cross on its grave as he had seen in cemeteries. The maid said that a cross was not appropriate because a bird was of a lower species than humans. The gatekeeper's son said the bird was Jewish, therefore there was no point in putting a cross on its grave, and in any case, the bird wouldn't go to heaven. Heaven was reserved for Christian saints, and the bird, just like Henryk himself, would at best go to a place where there was only darkness.

The Doctor said that at that time he was still afraid of the dark, and that from this conversation he learned two things, that he was Jewish, and that being Jewish seemed to be a problem.

When he was a teenager, his father got sick and was taken to hospital, where he died after a few years. The family had no income and Henryk had to go to work. He gave private lessons at school and decided to become a doctor.

"Why a doctor?" I asked.

"I wanted to help people," he explained, and he decided to help those who needed it most, the poor. He decided that he wanted to help those who were most deprived, the children of poor people. He told me about the conversations he had with street children, what he learned from them, about his battles, his crusades for the rights of children, that they should not be lowly creatures who only cause disturbances and must be trained like animals. He talked about the books he had written for children and adults, to help them understand children. He talked about the wars he had taken part in, about his visits to Palestine, about the upheavals in Poland, about justice and love.

When dawn broke and the first light entered the little attic, the Doctor said, "The day has begun, Janek, last question, please."

I asked him why he had abandoned medicine and chosen to take care of orphans.

He smiled a tired smile, "Because of you, because of children like you. You yourself are the answer."

And then he rose from the sofa, and as he did every morning, he opened the shutters and scattered bread crumbs on the window sill. The clear sky filled with birds fluttering towards him. He was my father.

Warsaw, Poland. 1939

AUTHOR'S NOTE

Janek Wolf, the main hero of this novel, is a fictional character, but Janusz Korczak and his orphanage were real. Hundreds of Jewish orphans grew up in this unique orphanage during the 30 years it existed in Warsaw, Poland, until World War II brought a terrible end to it.

For years I have wanted to write a book about Janusz Korczak, a revolutionary pedagogue, pediatrician, and writer who dedicated his life to children and their right to live in dignity. I decided to write and tell of this great man through a story that takes place in what was his greatest achievement: a democratic orphanage. Before I invented Janek, his family and friends, I needed to do extensive research and learn all I could about this extraordinary place and the life of its residents.

I read Korczak's pedagogy books for adults and his adventure books for children. I also read books written about him by educators and historians. I met two of Korczak's pupils, Izhak Belfer and Shlomo Nadel, who left the orphanage before the war broke out. They talked about Korczak and Miss Steffa with love and longing. Their stories and other stories about the orphanage, including those written by Korczak himself, served as an inspiration for this book.

For example, Belfer, who was allowed to use a small shop on the premises as an art studio, received paint, paper and crayons, without ever being asked to show results. He helped me get the details of life at the orphanage right. From the book by Paulina Apanshlak, *The Doctor Stayed*, I learned about the Doctor's work at the hospital on Szliska Street.

My story of Korczak is a mixture of fact and fiction. Most of the details regarding the children's court, the trials and the orphanage rules are real, but the first children's vote regarding a new ward took place three months after he or she was accepted. For the sake of plot momentum, I shortened Janek's probation period to only one month.

Shlomo Nadel was in charge of the cameras at the orphanage and grew up to be photographer. He told me the story about the camera he used to dream about, the Retina. In order to save money to buy it he would walk to visit his relatives, instead of taking the tram. He also told me about the carbon paper he once used in order to copy the many pages he had been assigned to copy as punishment in school. (Korczak was delighted with his initiative, finding a short cut to complete the task, as he thought it was a stupid punishment). Nadel's stories about the camera and the carbon paper helped me construct a plot appropriate for the period.

Janek's background and experiences are similar to those of many of the poor Jewish children of Warsaw at the time. I sent him to Korczak's orphanage in order to bring life to this special institution. I tried to build a plot which would be reflect the wonderful world that existed at 92 Krochmalna Street in Warsaw, and was considered by the hundreds of its young wards as a Garden of Eden for children.

MORE ABOUT JANUSZ KORCZAK

Janusz Korczak was born as Henryk (Hirsch) Goldszmit in Warsaw, Poland, on July 22nd 1878 or 1879 (According to UNESCO it was 1878).

Even as a child, Korczak was always aware of the suffering and misfortune of others. When walking with his father through the streets of Warsaw, he was saddened by the hard life of the poor, especially the children. The financial condition of his family was satisfactory during the first decade of his life but deteriorated when his father fell ill and was hospitalized for several years before he died. Korczak helped to support his family by giving private lessons.

When he was young, Korczak was not sure what he would do when he grew up. On the one hand he loved writing stories and dreamt of being a writer. He even sent a few stories to literary competitions and to newspapers; on one of them he signed his name as Janusz Korczak and the name stuck. On the other hand he wanted to do something useful, something that would be most beneficial for his fellow men. Finally he decided to study medicine; and if medicine, then pediatrics, for children were the weakest members of the society at the time.

He became a famous pediatrician; people knew that he could be called at all hours of the day or night and that he would come to see the small patient regardless if he or she lived in a slum or in a posh neighborhood. He never discriminated against the poor, on the contrary, he only collected fees from those who could afford them. Sometimes he even left money for food and medicines. Korczak could have been a rich man but money was of no interest to him. In addition to his occupation as a physician, Korczak wrote articles on education and books for children and adults.

In 1899, he visited Switzerland where he was exposed to various educational methods. Some years later, he accepted the position as a manager of an orphanage funded by a group of Jewish philanthropists. He was glad to discover that Steffa Wiltszinska was already involved in the project and he decided to give up medicine and devote himself to the administration of the orphanage. He always said that without her the orphanage could not have existed. He had the dream, but she was the one who made the dream come true. For long periods – sometimes for years – when Korczak was called up to serve as a military doctor during the war between Japan and Russia and also during the First World War, she managed the orphanage all on her own.

This was an unusual orphanage, run mainly by its children. They had a parliament of their own, a court of law, and their own newspaper. Every year, they would spend two months of the summer holiday in the country on a working farm where they would hold their own Olympic Games. Above all, everyone was treated with love and respect. At that time children, especially from poor families, could only dream of all this. When Poland became independent, Korczak established another orphanage for Christian children on the same principles. He was always sorry that the two institutions could not be combined.

As mentioned before, he wrote for adults as well as for children, books on pedagogy, plays and short stories, and articles in the newspapers. He also established a national children's newspaper. He lectured, spoke on the radio and gave evidence in courts of law. All this was for one purpose only: in order to improve the condition of children all over the world. He was one of the first to speak about the rights of children, that children should be protected by law from adults and from themselves. He had no private life and no property. He lived with the children in the orphanage.

In 1939, Poland was occupied by the Germans and the last three years of his life Korczak spent under Nazi rule. The orphanage was moved to a smaller building inside the Jewish Ghetto, and later into an even smaller place. During these years, though hungry and sick himself he took more and more children from the streets and gave them shelter. He collected firewood, scraps of food and medicine to keep them all warm and fed. It is a known fact that he could have saved his life more than once, but he refused to leave the children.

In August 1942, the Nazis began deporting the inhabitants of the Ghetto to Treblinka. Thousands were sent to their death, including 4,000 Jewish orphans from various orphanages. On August 5th, the Korczak orphanage was evacuated; 200 children, 10 teachers, and educators including Korczak himself and Steffa. Not one of them survived.

ABOUT THE AUTHOR

Tami Shem-Tov, born in Israel in 1969, is an award-winning writer for children and young readers. She writes mainly historical novels, biographies, and stories based on real events. She teaches creative writing in universities and libraries and meets children for talks about books and the power of stories to make a change. She lives in Tel-Aviv with her two daughters.

When We Had Wings is the first volume of a trilogy. The second volume is *When We Flew Away*. Tami Shem-Tov is currently writing the third part of this trilogy.

AMSTERDAM PUBLISHERS HOLOCAUST LIBRARY

The series **Holocaust Survivor Memoirs World War II** consists of the following autobiographies of survivors:

Outcry. Holocaust Memoirs, by Manny Steinberg

Hank Brodt Holocaust Memoirs. A Candle and a Promise, by Deborah Donnelly

The Dead Years. Holocaust Memoirs, by Joseph Schupack

Rescued from the Ashes. The Diary of Leokadia Schmidt, Survivor of the Warsaw Ghetto, by Leokadia Schmidt

My Lvov. Holocaust Memoir of a twelve-year-old Girl, by Janina Hescheles

Remembering Ravensbrück. From Holocaust to Healing, by Natalie Hess

Wolf. A Story of Hate, by Zeev Scheinwald with Ella Scheinwald

Save my Children. An Astonishing Tale of Survival and its Unlikely Hero, by Leon Kleiner with Edwin Stepp

Holocaust Memoirs of a Bergen-Belsen Survivor & Classmate of Anne Frank, by Nanette Blitz Konig

Defiant German - Defiant Jew. A Holocaust Memoir from inside the Third Reich, by Walter Leopold with Les Leopold

In a Land of Forest and Darkness. The Holocaust Story of two Jewish Partisans, by Sara Lustigman Omelinski

Holocaust Memories. Annihilation and Survival in Slovakia, by Paul Davidovits

From Auschwitz with Love. The Inspiring Memoir of Two Sisters' Survival, Devotion and Triumph Told by Manci Grunberger Beran & Ruth Grunberger Mermelstein, by Daniel Seymour

Remetz. Resistance Fighter and Survivor of the Warsaw Ghetto, by Jan Yohay Remetz

My March Through Hell. A Young Girl's Terrifying Journey to Survival, by Halina Kleiner with Edwin Stepp

Memoirs by Elmar Rivosh, Sculptor (1906-1967). Riga Ghetto and Beyond, by Elmar Rivosh

Roman's Journey, by Roman Halter

~

The series **Holocaust Survivor True Stories WWII** consists of the following biographies:

Among the Reeds. The true story of how a family survived the Holocaust, by Tammy Bottner

A Holocaust Memoir of Love & Resilience. Mama's Survival from Lithuania to America, by Ettie Zilber

Living among the Dead. My Grandmother's Holocaust Survival Story of Love and Strength, by Adena Bernstein Astrowsky

Heart Songs. A Holocaust Memoir, by Barbara Gilford

Shoes of the Shoah. The Tomorrow of Yesterday, by Dorothy Pierce

Hidden in Berlin. A Holocaust Memoir, by Evelyn Joseph Grossman

Separated Together. The Incredible True WWII Story of Soulmates Stranded an Ocean Apart, by Kenneth P. Price, Ph.D.

The Man Across the River. The incredible story of one man's will to survive the Holocaust, by Zvi Wiesenfeld

If Anyone Calls, Tell Them I Died. A Memoir, by Emanuel (Manu) Rosen

The House on Thrömerstrasse. A Story of Rebirth and Renewal in the Wake of the Holocaust, by Ron Vincent

Dancing with my Father. His hidden past. Her quest for truth. How Nazi Vienna shaped a family's identity, by Jo Sorochinsky

The Story Keeper. Weaving the Threads of Time and Memory - A Memoir, by Fred Feldman

Krisia's Silence. The Girl who was not on Schindler's List, by Ronny Hein

Defying Death on the Danube. A Holocaust Survival Story, by Debbie J. Callahan with Henry Stern

A Doorway to Heroism. A decorated German-Jewish Soldier who became an American Hero, by Rabbi W. Jack Romberg

The Shoemaker's Son. The Life of a Holocaust Resister, by Laura Beth Bakst

The Redhead of Auschwitz. A True Story, by Nechama Birnbaum

Land of Many Bridges. My Father's Story, by Bela Ruth Samuel Tenenholtz

Creating Beauty from the Abyss. The Amazing Story of Sam Herciger, Auschwitz Survivor and Artist, by Lesley Ann Richardson

On Sunny Days We Sang. A Holocaust Story of Survival and Resilience, by Jeannette Grunhaus de Gelman

Painful Joy. A Holocaust Family Memoir, by Max J. Friedman

I Give You My Heart. A True Story of Courage and Survival, by Wendy Holden

In the Time of Madmen, by Mark A. Prelas

Monsters and Miracles. Horror, Heroes and the Holocaust, by Ira Wesley Kitmacher

Flower of Vlora. Growing up Jewish in Communist Albania, by Anna Kohen

Aftermath: Coming of Age on Three Continents. A Memoir, by Annette Libeskind Berkovits

Not a real Enemy. The True Story of a Hungarian Jewish Man's Fight for Freedom, by Robert Wolf

Zaidy's War. Four Armies, Three Continents, Two Brothers. One Man's Impossible Story of Endurance, by Martin Bodek

The Glassmaker's Son. Looking for the World my Father left behind in Nazi Germany, by Peter Kupfer

The Apprentice of Buchenwald. The True Story of the Teenage Boy Who Sabotaged Hitler's War Machine, by Oren Schneider

Burying the Ghosts, by Sonia Case

American Wolf. From Nazi Refugee to American Spy. A True Story, by Audrey Birnbaum

Bipolar Refugee. A Saga of Survival and Resilience, by Peter Wiesner

~

The series **Jewish Children in the Holocaust** consists of the following autobiographies of Jewish children hidden during WWII in the Netherlands:

Searching for Home. The Impact of WWII on a Hidden Child, by Joseph Gosler

See You Tonight and Promise to be a Good Boy! War memories, by Salo Muller

Sounds from Silence. Reflections of a Child Holocaust Survivor, Psychiatrist and Teacher, by Robert Krell

Sabine's Odyssey. A Hidden Child and her Dutch Rescuers, by Agnes Schipper

The Journey of a Hidden Child, by Harry Pila and Robin Black

The series **New Jewish Fiction** consists of the following novels, written by Jewish authors. All novels are set in the time during or after the Holocaust.

The Corset Maker. A Novel, by Annette Libeskind Berkovits

Escaping the Whale. The Holocaust is over. But is it ever over for the next generation? by Ruth Rotkowitz

When the Music Stopped. Willy Rosen's Holocaust, by Casey Hayes

Hands of Gold. One Man's Quest to Find the Silver Lining in Misfortune, by Roni Robbins

The Girl Who Counted Numbers. A Novel, by Roslyn Bernstein

There was a garden in Nuremberg. A Novel, by Navina Michal Clemerson

The Butterfly and the Axe, by Omer Bartov

To Live Another Day. A Novel, Elizabeth Rosenberg

Good for a Single Journey, by Helen Joyce

~

The series **Holocaust Heritage** consists of the following memoirs by 2G:

The Silk Factory: Finding Threads of My Family's True Holocaust Story, by Michael Hickins

The Cello Still Sings. A Generational Story of the Holocaust and of the Transformative Power of Music, by Janet Horvath

The Fire and the Bonfire. A journey into memory, by Ardyn Halter

~

The series **Holocaust Books for Young Adults** consists of the following novels, based on true stories:

The Boy behind the Door. How Salomon Kool Escaped the Nazis. Inspired by a True Story, by David Tabatsky

Running for Shelter. A True Story, by Suzette Sheft

The Precious Few. An Inspirational Saga of Courage based on True Stories, by David Twain with Art Twain

Jacob's Courage: A Holocaust Love Story, by Charles S. Weinblatt

~

The series **WW2 Historical Fiction** consists of the following novels, some of which are based on true stories:

Mendelevski's Box. A Heartwarming and Heartbreaking Jewish Survivor's Story, by Roger Swindells

A Quiet Genocide. The Untold Holocaust of Disabled Children WW2 Germany, by Glenn Bryant

The Knife-Edge Path, by Patrick T. Leahy

Brave Face. The Inspiring WWII Memoir of a Dutch/German Child, by I. Caroline Crocker and Meta A. Evenbly

When We Had Wings. The Gripping Story of an Orphan in Janusz Korczak's Orphanage. A Historical Novel, by Tami Shem-Tov

Want to be an AP book reviewer?

Reviews are very important in a world dominated by the social media and social proof. Please drop us a line if you want to join the *AP review team*.
info@amsterdampublishers.com